CU00705427

TRUMPED
AN ALTERNATIVE MUSICAL

This edition first published in 2020 by Blue Lens
Blue Lens is an imprint of Blue Lens Films Limited

Blue Lens Films Limited, 71-75 Shelton Street,
Covent Garden, London, WC2H 9JQ, United Kingdom

Text copyright © Ben Fletcher 2018-2020
Text Copyright © Brianna Bennett 2018-2020
Cover design © Toupee or Not Toupee Limited

This book contains material which parodies the work of
other authors and/or creators. Such parties are permitted
under Section 107 of the Copyright Act (United States)
and similar laws in other territories and jurisdictions.

The moral right of the author to be identified as the
creator of this work has been asserted under the Copyright,
Design, and Patents Act 1988 (UK)

All rights reserved. This book is sold subject to the
condition that it shall not, by way of trade or otherwise,
be lent, resold, hired, copied, or otherwise circulated in
any form of binding or cover, in part or entirety, without
the prior written consent of the publisher and Toupee or
Not Toupee Limited, except where license is granted.

Although parodying true events, TRUMPED: An Alternative
Musical should not be considered a true or accurate record
or representation of those events, nor should it be
considered an accurate portrayal of the people satirized
within.

ISBN 978 1 913408 95 4
1 3 5 9 10 8 6 4 2

Printer and binder may vary between territories of
production and sale

LICENSE INFORMATION

Subject to the terms and conditions set out in this book, the purchase* of this book entitles you to be granted a one-time non-transferable performance license for the material with the following conditions:

VERSION	TRUMPED: An Alternative Musical, Part One (Act I & II)
LICENSE TYPE	Amateur One Performance *See terms for eligibility criteria*
LICENSE AREA	Australia, Canada, European Economic Area, New Zealand, South Africa, United Kingdom, United States
NUMBER OF PERFORMANCES	Maximum of one performance
MAXIMUM AUDIENCE	Not to exceed 150 in aggregate
TICKET PRICE RESTRICTIONS	Not to exceed USD 10.00 (or foreign equivalent) per ticket, or USD 900 (or foreign equivalent) in aggregate.

*Only the first purchaser of this book is entitled to be granted a performance license. Used or resold copies do not entitle you to a performance license.

To register for your license, please complete the online for at analternativemusical.com/performancelicenses.

TERMS OF LICENSE

1) Subject to these terms, the first purchaser of this book ("the licensee") (defined as the individual/ organization to first purchase this copy from a recognized registered book retailer), is entitled to be granted by Toupee or Not Toupee Limited (a UK based company managing the rights to TRUMPED: An Alternative Musical on behalf of the rights holders), a one-time non-transferable performance or use license for the material contained within this book.

2) No performance license will be granted for purchasers of used or resold copies of this book.

3) No performance or performance-related work may begin until a performance license has been granted to the licensee.

4) The granting of a performance license is subject to the successful registration of the licensee and their purchase of this book. Satisfactory proof of first purchase is required before a license is granted.

5) Licensees can register their book purchase at analternativemusical.com/performancelicenses.

6) The license must register before January 1, 2022. No license will be granted for registrations after this date. All licenses (except educational use) will be valid for a period of twelve months. Any and all performance-related work and performances must take place within this period. Educational use licenses will be valid for a period of three months. Any use, performance-related work or performances undertaken outside of this period will be deemed unlicensed use.

7) Licenses will be granted subject to the terms and with the conditions as set out within this book. License terms or conditions will not be varied under any circumstance.

8) Only one license will be granted per book and each licensee is limited to a maximum of five licenses.

9) Educational licenses are available only to registered non-profit educational organizations within the license area.

10) Non-profit licenses are available only to registered non-profit organizations within the license area.

11) Amateur licensees are available only to amateur performance groups within the license area and with annual revenues not exceeding USD 25,000 (or foreign equivalent) in the previous financial year.

12) Licenses are valid only within the license area, defined as: The United States, United Kingdom, European Economic Area, Canada, Australia, New Zealand, and South Africa.

13) Once a purchase is registered, a license cannot be canceled for any reason.

14) Once a license is granted, the licensee is required to enter the license number on each page of this book in the designated area, after which, copies of the material may be made in order to distribute for performance or education use as the license allows. No copying is permitted without a license number being entered on each page. Licensees are required to control and note the number of copies of the material being made. All copies must be returned to the licensee and destroyed at the end of the material's licensed use.

15) Once licensed, subject to the conditions of that license and these terms, the licensee is permitted to produce the material contained within this book for public performance. This does not apply to educational use licenses which grant the license to use the material in a purely educational environment with performances permitted to non-paying audiences not exceeding 30 persons.

16) Licensees must produce the material in full with no edits of any kind (substitutions, additions or subtractions) permitted. In the circumstance of extract licenses, the licensee is permitted to choose up to fifteen scenes to produced. These scenes must be produced in full with no edits of any kind (substitutions, additions or subtractions) permitted.

17) Performances must take place at a premises which is owned and/or controlled by the licensee. No performances may take place as part of a festival in any territory or within 50 miles of a city where a current arts festival is taking place during that festival.

18) No additional rights, including, but not limited to, artwork, likeness, trademarks (registered or otherwise), or any other intellectual property is included as part of any license. No license is granted for any music, tune, incidental music, or any other material which may, in some circumstances, be held by third party rights holders.

19) Licensees are required to observe all relevant local, state, and national laws, and any relevant union agreement. Under no circumstances will the retailer, distributor, publisher, Toupee or Not Toupee Limited, the

rights holders, or any other third party be liable to the licensee or any person, group, or organization associated with the licensee, for any loss or liability which the licensee experiences or which is incurred as a result of a license being granted.

20) In no circumstance will the livability of the retailer, distributor, publisher, Toupee or Not Toupee Limited, the rights holders, or any other third party be liable to the licensee or any person, group, or organization associated with the licensee, exceed the United States list price of this book at the time of purchase.

21) For performances taking place in the United Kingdom or the European Economic Area, the licensee may be required to pay VAT in addition to the purchase of this book. No performance license will be granted until this is paid.

22) The licensee and any person, group, or organization associated with the licensee, must not bring the the retailer, distributor, publisher, Toupee or Not Toupee Limited, the rights holders, or any other third party into disrepute. This includes, but is not limited to, by sharing hateful messages and/or content, and using the licensed material in any way except that explicitly permitted in their license. Should Toupee or Not Toupee Limited decide that the licensee or any person, group, or organization associated with the licensee has breached this term, the license granted will be revoked without compensation to the licensee.

23) The licensee must ensure that they do not associate themselves or lead any person to believe they are associated with the retailer, distributor, publisher, Toupee or Not Toupee Limited, the rights holders, or any other third party.

24) Should the purchaser of this book be ineligible for a license, no refund of this book will be given. Should the licensee breach any term or condition of the license, the license granted will be revoked without compensation to the licensee.

INTRODUCTION

Written in four acts presented across two parts, TRUMPED:
An Alternative Musical is a satirical stage play that
parodies the 2016 Presidential Election campaign of Donald
Trump and his subsequent time in office as the 45th
President of the United States.

Opening on the final day of the July 2016 Republican
National Convention in Cleveland, Ohio, Act I tells the
story behind the Trump campaign's journey from the outsider
of the Republican field to the unexpected winner of the
Electoral College with a questionable victory.

Covering the Russia meeting at Trump Tower, all three
election debates against the Democratic opponent, Hillary
Clinton, and the attempts of the Russian President,
Vladimir Putin, to ensure a win for the Trump campaign in
the state of Wisconsin, Act I concludes at the end of
November 8, election day, as the final results come in.

With the election over and Donald Trump set to become the
4th President, Act II opens the day following the election
as both the world and the current President, Barack Obama,
are all still in shock at the previous day's result.

Concluding toward the end of Trump's first year in office,
Act II covers his and his Vice President, Mike Pence's
inaugurations, a visit to the White House by his German
counterpart, Angela Merkel, and the apparent early collapse
of the Trump regime brought about through the actions of
Robert Mueller, the tweets of Donald Trump Junior, and the
gullibility of Eric Trump, forcing the family to make a
quick escape and leave another to fall in their place as
Part One comes to a close.

Picking up some weeks after the conclusion of Part One, Act
III opens as the President is presumed missing by his
closet supporters, and Vladimir Putin is becoming tiresome
of ruling from the front lines.

With the job of bringing Trump back to the United States
tasked to him, Fox News anchor, Sean Hannity, soon sets off
to South America to discover that his journey home is to

(CONTINUED)

CONTINUED:

be hindered by the measures he supported.

Coming to a close as the 2018 Midterm elections approach,
Act III follows the President as, despite his America-first
attitude, he attempts to forge new international ties with
world leaders and royalty alike, while domestically, his
party works to secure a new seat on the Supreme Court.

Act IV opens with an opportunity to discover how Trump's
predecessor is coping with his post-presidential life and
his thoughts on the upcoming Midterm elections. Leaving
island life behind, the action then returns to Trump as he
discovers that under his leadership, the Republican Party
is set for a historic loss.

Following the Midterms being brought to you live from
Florida and Texas, Act IV goes on to tell the story of a
government shutdown and fine dining Trump-style as the
Democrats begin searching for their 2020 nominee.

Coming to a close in late 2019, this final act builds up to
an interpretation of events as they should have been, with
the President finally being held to account.

CAST OF CHARACTERS

All characters are listed in order of appearance.

HILLARY CLINTON, Presidential Candidate/ Former Sec. State
DONALD TRUMP, Presidential Candidate/ 45th President
MICHAEL COHEN, Lawyer to Donald Trump
KELLYANNE CONWAY, Campaign Manager to Donald Trump
STEPHEN MILLER, Advisor to Donald Trump
NYT JOURNALIST, Journalist from the New York Times
THE NARRATOR, Narrator of TRUMPED: An Alternative Musical
DONALD TRUMP JR, Son to Donald Trump
IVANKA TRUMP, Daughter to Donald Trump
ERIC TRUMP, Son to Donald Trump/ Eric
LAWYER, Lawyer to the Narrator
MIKE PENCE, Running Mate to Donald Trump/ Vice-President
JARED KUSHNER, Son-in-Law and Advisor to Donald Trump
VLADIMIR PUTIN, President of Russia/ American Supreme Ruler
DELIVERY DRIVER, Takeout Delivery Driver
CHRIS CHRISTIE, Governor of New Jersey
DMITRY SUREFIRE, Agent of the Kremlin
PETROV SUREFIRE, Agent of the Kremlin
RUDY GIULIANI, Former NYC Mayor/ Lawyer to Donald Trump
LESTER HOLT, NBC News Anchor/ First Debate Moderator
CLINTON AIDE, Aide to Hillary Clinton
TIM KAINE, Running Mate to Hillary Clinton
MIDWESTERN VOTER, Voter from the Midwest
BILL CLINTON, 42nd President/ Husband to Hillary Clinton
ANDERSON COOPER, CNN News Anchor/ Second Debate Moderator
MARTHA RADDATZ, ABC News Anchor/ Second Debate Moderator
BARACK OBAMA, 44th President
MICHELLE OBAMA, First Lady
BERNIE SANDERS, Senator from Vermont/ Democratic Candidate
JOHN OLIVER, TV Host/ Comedian
MIKE HUCKABEE, Former Governor of Arkansas
SARAH PALIN, Former Governor of Alaska
CHRISTOPHER WALLACE, Fox Anchor/ Third Debate Moderator
RECORDED MESSAGE, Trump Grill Phone Message
ELECTION OFFICIAL, Election Official
STEVE DOOCY, Fox & Friends Host
AINSLEY EARHARDT, Fox & Friends Host
BRIAN KILMEADE, Fox & Friends Host
WISCONSIN VOTER, Voter from Wisconsin
SEAN HANNITY, Fox News Anchor

(CONTINUED)

CONTINUED:

PRESS #1, CNN Journalist
PRESS #2, New York Times Journalist
PRESS #3, Washington Post Journalist
PRESS #4, NBC Journalist
PRESS #5, Fox News Journalist
PRESS #6, MSNBC Journalist
SEAN SPICER, White House Press Secretary
ANGELA MERKEL, Chancellor of Germany
PAUL RYAN, Speaker of the House
PRODUCTION ASSISTANT, Assistant to Anderson Cooper
DAY CARE ASSISTANT, White House Day Care Assistant
ANTHONY SCARAMUCCI, Director of Communications
SARAH HUCKABEE SANDERS, White House Press Secretary
DELIVERY MAN #1, White House Delivery Worker
DELIVERY MAN #2, White House Delivery Worker
FBI AGENT #1, Agent for the FBI
FBI AGENT #2, Agent for the FBI
ROBERT MUELLER, Former FBI Director/ Special Counsel
CHECK-IN AGENT, Airport Check-In Agent

PRODUCTION NOTES

At all performances, the production crew should ensure that a message is played to audiences in order to inform them that while based upon and satirizing true events, TRUMPED: An Alternative Musical, Part One and Two, should not be considered a true or accurate record or representation of those events, nor should it be considered to portray the individuals satirized within accurately.

At all performances, a seat should be resaved at the end of the row within the audience for the character of Hillary Clinton to make her entrance from in Act I, Scene 7. This seat should be within the front orchestra section and be viewable, as far as reasonably possible, by all sections of the auditorium.

To cover the high number of characters within TRUMPED: An Alternative Musical, the majority of company members should perform multiple roles. This excludes the company member who is playing the role of the Narrator.

Where the script refers to the Ensemble, this should be taken to mean all company members, who are available at the time of that scene (i.e., not performing a different role within the scene or undertaking a wardrobe change), except for where specific exemptions are noted within the script.

The note that follows the introduction of the ensemble provides additional information on the role which the ensemble is performing in that scene (e.g., "ENSEMBLE (as PRESS").

In some instances, specific characters will be included as part of the ensemble (e.g., "Press #1").

At no point should company members performing the role of the Narrator or Donald Trump be included within the ensemble.

Performances of TRUMPED: An Alternative Musical should not require additional ensemble members outside of principal company members and understudies.

(CONTINUED)

CONTINUED:

The role of the Narrator is nonspecific for casting
purposes, and freedom should be offered to this company
member to perform their own style of narration (within the
direction of the written material and director).

With the majority of characters in TRUMPED: An Alternative
Musical based upon real people and to be performed as
impersonations and parodies, company members should be
given the freedom (within the direction of the written
material and director) to perform the impersonation as they
feel most appropriate. This may include the changing of
minor words, the mispronunciation of words and phrases, or
varying the pace of delivery.

"Cardboard Melania" should be achieved through the creation
of a life-size cardboard cutout of Melania Trump being
attached to an RC vehicle, which is controlled from
offstage.

<u>Dialogue</u>   Indicates that dialogue should be
                  mispronounced.

Dialogue   Indicates that dialogue should be
                  emphasized.

/DIALOGUE/   Indicates that dialogue should be sung.

PART ONE

ACT I : "THE CAMPAIGN"

ACT I, PRE-SHOW | PRE-SHOW

>   On an otherwise empty and dark
>   stage, a dimly lit flagpole
>   stands front stage right with a
>   United States flag moving gently
>   in a wind that comes from
>   somewhere offstage.
>
>   With the audience seated, the
>   lights in the auditorium go down
>   to leave the flag as the only
>   thing in the room that's lit.

                         CLINTON (PRE-RECORDED)
Well, hello there, everyone. I'm Hillary Rodham Clinton,
and I'm here to thank you for coming to watch this here
performance of 'Trumped: An Alternative Musical' today, or
as I sometimes call it, fifty shades of orange.

Incidentally, did you happen to know that I've been to see
shows like this one many times myself before? Going to the
theater is a thing that people do, and I'm a people. I'm
Hillary Rodham Clinton, and I'm relatable. You could even
say that I'm Hillary Relatable Clinton.

So before we begin the performance, I would just like to
give you a quick reminder that all forms of electronic
devices and phones should be switched off now for the
duration of the performance. Did you know that I still use
a Blackberry personally? It does everything I need it too.
My calls, my messages and, of course, all of my em --
electronic letters.

I know what you're saying, "typical Hillary, spoiling all
the fun for us," but I say if for everyone's benefit, just
like when I warned you all about Bernie Sanders.
                              (MORE)

                                              (CONTINUED)

CONTINUED:

> CLINTON (PRE-RECORDED) (CONT'D)
> Those texts and those calls can wait until after the show for you, and as for your emails, well, they can wait even longer. We don't need to worry about the emails. We never need to worry about the emails.
>
> Thank you for your co-operation and enjoy the show.

ACT I, SCENE ONE | THE REPUBLICAN NATIONAL CONVENTION

> In a CONFERENCE HALL in Ohio, the flag remains the only thing lit as we begin to hear the voices of a conversation from backstage.

> TRUMP (OFF)
> Do you promise me, lawyer man, that if I sign this document here, nobody will ever find out?

> COHEN (OFF)
> Of course, Mister Trump. It's a non-disclosure agreement. It's an effective way of keeping things, and people, that should be kept quiet, quiet, if you know what I mean, boss?

> TRUMP (OFF)
> And all I have to do is sign my name here?

> COHEN (OFF)
> Almost, boss. You sign your name on the line, but you also need to sort out the money to pay them off too.

> TRUMP (OFF)
> And how much is this one?

> COHEN (OFF)
> One hundred and thirty thousand dollars.

> TRUMP (OFF)
> Can you sort out the money? I will pay you back one day in the future, probably.

> COHEN (OFF)
> Are you sure, sir?

(CONTINUED)

CONTINUED:

                         TRUMP (OFF)
Of course, I am sure, Michael Cohen. You can trust me. I am
the most trustworthy person that you know.

                         COHEN (OFF)
Well okay, if you're certain. But what about the signature
though, boss?

                         TRUMP (OFF)
That will have to wait. I have to go on stage to talk to a
bunch of losers right now.

                         COHEN (OFF)
But it only takes a second to sign.

                         TRUMP (OFF)
I have to find the correct spelling before I can sign it.

                         COHEN (OFF)
Okay, boss. But don't forget to sign it, the entire
agreement would be worthless if you do. You don't know how
it might come back on you.

                         TRUMP (OFF)
Do not worry yourself, I would never be that stupid.

                         COHEN (OFF)
I believe you, boss. Well, I'd love to stay and watch your
big speech, but Sean Hannity wanted to see me about
something. Good luck.

                              Silence falls before the United
                              States National Anthem begins to
                              play, and a podium appears next
                              to the flag.

                              A moment later, TRUMP enters and
                              stands behind the podium as the
                              music stops.

                         TRUMP
Privet, mo kollegi-Amerikantsy --

                                              (CONTINUED)
PERFORMANCE LICENSE EDITION   LICENSE # _ _ _ _ _ _ _

CONTINUED:

                              KELLYANNE CONWAY runs on stage
                              in a panic and whispers in his
                              ear.

                    TRUMP
Thank you for letting me know that, Kellyanne Conway.

                    CONWAY exits.

                    TRUMP
Friends, delegates, and fellow Americans, except for those
who look foreign even though they are not, by the way, I am
the most American person you have ever met. Trust me, okay
folks.

Anyway, I, Donald J. Trump, do hereby right now accept
humblebee... no, Huckabee... no, humbly accept, because I
am a very humble man, your nomination for the Presidency of
the United States...

                              He trails off into a silent mime
                              as lights find CONWAY and
                              STEPHEN MILLER watching from
                              across the stage.

                    MILLER
Such elegance in all of his words.

                    CONWAY
Isn't there?

                    MILLER
And he's finally speaking in English too.

                    TRUMP
I loves these uniqueded swates of awericma!

                    MILLER
Well, almost.

                    CONWAY
He was reluctant for a while, but I just told him that
English is alternative Russian, and he went with it.

                                              (CONTINUED)

                        Unnoticed, an NYT JOURNALIST
                        enters and begins taking notes
                        behind them.

                        MILLER
How is that going? Teaching him Russian, I mean.

                        CONWAY
It's going really well. He says that Russian is his new
language of love.

                        MILLER
Let me tell you what I think for a moment. I think it's
quite annoying. We should have just colluded with a country
that speaks English.

                        CONWAY
Because none of those countries like us.

                        MILLER
                        (nodding)
Fair point. How is the collusion going?

                        CONWAY
It's going okay. The Russians can give us some real help.
We haven't told Mike about everything that's going on yet,
though.

                        MILLER
What haven't you told him?

                        CONWAY
We thought it would be best not to tell him everything
about all the help Russia is giving Mister Trump.

                        MILLER
Why not?

                        CONWAY
Well, Mike is just a little old-fashioned...

                        MILLER looks at her perplexed.

                                    (CONTINUED)

CONTINUED:

                    CONWAY
We don't know if he actually approves of treason.

                                        MILLER glances back at her as
                                        the NYT JOURNALIST sneezes,
                                        prompting them both to look.

                    CONWAY
Who are you?

                    NYT JOURNALIST
Oh... I'm just --

                    MILLER
Let me speak for a moment. I know who you are. I've seen
you before. You work for the New York Times.

                    CONWAY
The New York Times? You're a journalist? But we don't like
journalists do we, Stephen?

                    MILLER
How much of our conversation did you just overhear?

                    CONWAY
Did you overhear the bit when I said that the Trump
campaign is actively colluding with the Russian Government
in order to fix the election?
                    (beat)
Because you shouldn't know about that.

                                        A pause, and then a flash of a
                                        camera as the NYT JOURNALIST
                                        takes a photo of them.

                                        CONWAY and MILLER step closer.

                    NYT JOURNALIST
Please, have mercy on me. Just let me go. I've got two
children.

                                        Another step closer.

                                                        (CONTINUED)

                            MILLER
We're Republicans. We don't care about the children.

                                    As they take another step
                                    closer, at the front of the
                                    stage, TRUMP begins to hug the
                                    flagpole.

                            NYT JOURNALIST
                        (noticing TRUMP)
What is he doing?

                                    CONWAY and MILLER look at TRUMP.

                            MILLER
Oh my Comrade Putin...

                            CONWAY
He's hugging the flag again.
                        (to NYT JOURNALIST)
You wait here for us. We'll deal with you in a moment.

                                    As CONWAY and MILLER move to
                                    push TRUMP and the flag
                                    offstage, the NYT JOURNALIST
                                    takes another photo then makes a
                                    run for it.

ACT I, SCENE TWO | THE JOURNEY TO NEW YORK

                                    Aboard HAIR FORCE ONE in the
                                    main cabin of TRUMP's private
                                    jet where he paces up and down
                                    while CONWAY, ERIC TRUMP, IVANKA
                                    TRUMP, DONALD TRUMP JUNIOR,
                                    JARED KUSHNER, and MIKE PENCE,
                                    sit watching him.

                            NARRATOR
                        (entering)
And so it is to be that on July eighteen, two thousand and
sixteen, Donald Trump becomes the Republican --

                                                    (CONTINUED)

TRUMP

It's Donald J. Trump. Not Donald Trump. The J is important.
It stands for Jenius.

NARRATOR

And so it is to be that on July eighteen, two thousand and
sixteen, Donald...

TRUMP

J...

NARRATOR

Trump becomes the Republican candidate for the Presidency
of the United States of America. A historic moment, for it
marks the first time a person orange in color has received
such a nomination, a feat that could only have come about
with the help of Russia --

A LAWYER enters and coughs.

NARRATOR

Allegedly.

The LAWYER nods then exits.

NARRATOR

But the election is still many months away, and there's
still much for old Donald to do, for still he is yet to
battle, debate and argue with both Hillary Clinton and with
all of you.

So with his spray tan at the ready and his chief of staff
his former caddy, there's a campaign ahead, and in
preparation, both Steve Bannon and Chris Christie have been
fed.

It's time to hit the trail, all expecting them to fail. But
first, we journey to New York, for more than just so Mister
Trump can eat his K-F-C with a fork.

The NARRATOR exits.

(CONTINUED)

                          TRUMP
I think I have managed to get away with it. With Russia's
help, I am now the presidential candidate of the Russian
National Convention --

                          CONWAY
No! Mister Trump, sir. It's the Republican National
Convention.

                          TRUMP
Republican? But they were the people I once called the
dumbest bunch of voters in the country.

                          CONWAY
Yes, that's them, sir. But it won't matter, they're all too
dumb to remember that you said it.

                          TRUMP
I am confused. What is the Russian National Convention,
Kellyanne Conway?

                          CONWAY
That doesn't exist, sir.

                          TRUMP
Oh, does it not? Never mind then. Mike Pence, where are
you, Mike Pence?

                          PENCE
I'm right here, sir.

                          TRUMP
Okay, join me, Mike Pence.

                    PENCE joins him pacing.

                          PENCE
Mister Trump, why exactly are we doing this, sir?

                          TRUMP
We are doing this, Mike Pence, because this is what people
call walking and talking, and as we know, both bits, both
the walking and also the talking too, is what my favorite
president is famous for doing.

                                              (CONTINUED)

                         PENCE
And who is your favorite president, Mister Trump?

                         TRUMP
My favorite president, Mike Pence, is President Mister
Martin Sheen, Mike Pence. I can relate to him. Much like
me, he did not win the Emmy that he deserved, but also, the
thing that we have most in common is that no matter how
realistic it might look if I win, people will never believe
I am a real president.

                    Beat.

                         PENCE
You were truly robbed of that Emmy, sir.

                         TRUMP
Thank you, Mike Pence. I like you, Mike Pence.

Clearly, you have a lot of intelligent in you, and it is
such intelligence insight like that which is why I chose
for you to have the honor of being my walking mate.

                         PENCE
Your walking mate, sir?

                         TRUMP
Yes, Mike Pence. My walking mate. A walking mate is just
like a running mate, only it requires less exercise.

                         PENCE
Well, thank you, sir. It really is an honor to be chosen by
you.

                         TRUMP
You may sit now, Mike Pence.

                    PENCE sits.

                         JUNIOR
Hey dad, me and...

                         ERIC
Eric...

                                        (CONTINUED)

CONTINUED:

> JUNIOR
> We're both wondering, why are we going back to New York?
> Don't we need to be hitting the campaign trail straight
> away?

> TRUMP
> We are going back to New York, Donald Trump Junior, because
> we need to get our campaign team together and work out a
> strategy.
>
> I never actually thought I was going to win the nomination,
> not even I thought the Republican party would be this
> stupid, and so I never planned a campaign.
>
> I do know that I need you and Eric Trump to be there with
> me, though.

> ERIC
> Hey, it's not Eric. It's Eric.

> JUNIOR
> Thanks, dad. It's nice to know that you really value us.

> TRUMP
> Oh, it is not that, Donald Trump Junior. It is that you are
> both stupid enough to do all of the really illegal things
> for me.

> ERIC
> I'm stupid.

> TRUMP
> We were going to say in Ohio and meet at the end of the
> convention, but Chris Christie wanted to be there too, and
> as we all know, he is illegal in forty-six states.

> ERIC
> My name is Edward.

> CONWAY
> Mister Trump, if I may make a suggestion? Perhaps you
> should spend this journey coming up with some policy ideas?

                                                    (CONTINUED)

                         TRUMP
That is a very great idea, Kellyanne Conway. But I have a
better one.

                         CONWAY
What is your idea, sir?

                         TRUMP
I am going to spend this journey, this one that we are all
on now, coming up with some policy ideas.

                         IVANKA
Daddy.

                         TRUMP
Yes, darling?

                         IVANKA
I think that you should work on a policy that helps out
women who struggle.

                         CONWAY
Melania suggested that, but Donald said he doesn't want a
divorce. Where is Melania anyway?

                         TRUMP
She said she had a doctor's appointment.
                    (to IVANKA)
I like your idea, babycakes. Stand up and come to me so
that daddy can kiss you.

                              IVANKA stands and approaches
                              until the NARRATOR runs on and
                              gets in the way to end up being
                              kissed on the cheek by TRUMP.

                              There's a pause before the
                              NARRATOR wipes their face.

                         NARRATOR
This is supposed to be a family show. We're not going
there.
                    (beat)
                    (MORE)

                                              (CONTINUED)

CONTINUED:
                          NARRATOR (CONT'D)
But Ivanka has a point, because like it or not, and Donald
certainly doesn't, women are entitled to vote --

                          JUNIOR
I don't think it's a good idea either, and neither does
Eric, do you, buddy?

                          ERIC
What's a woman?

                          NARRATOR
And as such, they do need policies to appeal to the group
that few of them know. Unfortunately for the campaign,
Donald Trump is not a man who knows what appeals to women.

                          TRUMP
How does this sound, Ivanka Trump darling? Each and every
woman in America will be given, for free, a calendar where
me, Steve Bannon, and Mike Pence all dress up and pose as
firemen.

                          IVANKA
No.

                          CONWAY
Definitely not.

                          TRUMP
What would be wrong with it? It would be so great. Just so
great.

                          CONWAY
Two things. The first being Steve, and the second being
Bannon.

                          NARRATOR
And so with his first idea out, Trump begins to think,
until eventually inside his head, a light begins to blink.

                          TRUMP
I have got it. A genius idea. I am telling you all, this is
a genius idea. I am going to invent a new sort of pant that
will be made, and this is the really genius part, just for
women.

                                                (CONTINUED)

                         CONWAY
Sir?

                         TRUMP
Also, and this is the bit that will really blow all of your
minds so hold on to your toupees and your g-strings --

                         ERIC
But I don't own a guitar.

                         TRUMP
These pants will be called three quarters in length pants,
and they will, you would never have been able to guess
this, be three quarters the length of men's pants.

                         CONWAY
Mister Trump, sir?

                         TRUMP
Not now, Kellyanne Conway... These pants are going to also
cost, this is genius, three quarters the price of men's
pants.

There, your minds are all so blown, just so blown. I have
just solved the issue of women earning less. All women will
now be able to buy cheaper and shorter pants, because as we
all know, women all earn less and are shorter, except for
those who are not, but they are just losers.

Also, these new pants will all be beige and two sizes too
small.

                       A pause.

                         JUNIOR
                  (breaking the silence)
Well, I for one think that you've got a really good idea,
dad. I can't wait to see them come off.

                         TRUMP
Spoken just like your father, Donald Trump Junior.

                                              (CONTINUED)

CONTINUED:

                          JUNIOR
I think we could have them produced in foreign sweatshops
too. I know Ivanka has some. Not only would it save money,
but we'd be contributing to foreign aid.

                          TRUMP
I like your thinking there. What do you think, Jared
Kushner?

                    KUSHNER remains silent.

                          IVANKA
Jared?

                    Again, he's silent.

                          TRUMP
That guy is always quiet. That is why I like him. A guy who
is quiet cannot leak.
                         (beat)
Anyway, I am certain all women will have to thank me for
this invention. If they do not, then they are just mean and
sexist.

                          ERIC
I met a woman once. She came close to me and my Eric grew.
She's Missus Eric now.

                          IVANKA
Your Eric?

                          ERIC
My Eric, that's right. I have an Eric, so does dad, and
Junior too.

                          IVANKA
What do I have then?

                          ERIC
Oh, you? You have a Missus Eric.

                          IVANKA
Missus Eric? Are you talking about your wife?

                                              (CONTINUED)

                              ERIC
That's right, Missus Eric. Have you met her? She's just
like me except she has man boobs like dad.

                              Beat.

                            NARRATOR
While there is one idea down, there is still many more to
come, and nothing is off the table, from the bad.

                             TRUMP
How about we deport anyone who speaks more than one
language for showing disrespect to the American language...
English.

                            NARRATOR
To the very bad.

                             TRUMP
Or how about we force every newborn child to be called
Donald Trump in my honor?

                            NARRATOR
To how did this guy actually get the nomination?

                                   VLADIMIR PUTIN crosses the back
                                   of the stage unnoticed.

                             TRUMP
We should create an American monarchy.

                            NARRATOR
Ideas were shared and thrown around until the journey to
New York has in full been flown, Eric excluded, of course,
for he needed a prop to be entertained, a hat that allowed
him to pretend to fly the plane.

                                   JUNIOR places a pilot's hat onto
                                   ERIC.

                              ERIC
Welcome aboard this Eric Airlines flight E-R-I-C to
Ericville. I am your pilot, Eric.
                             (MORE)

PERFORMANCE LICENSE EDITION   LICENSE # _ _ _ _ _ _ _ _

                              ERIC (CONT'D)
                    (beat)
This is so cool!

ACT I, SCENE THREE | CONWAY & CHRISTIE

                              TRUMP'S OFFICE in Trump Tower
                              where a desk sits waiting and
                              nearby, tall curtains hang.

                              NARRATOR
And so before long, we arrive in New York, landing on the
tarmac runway four at LaGuardia airport. And as we arrive,
the cars are waiting to take the family to Midtown for
meetings of much anticipating. For on the corner of Fifth
and Fifty-Sixth stands tall the fifty-eight stories of
Trump --

                              TRUMP enters while eating from a
                              box of chicken.

                              TRUMP
No. It is actually sixty-eight stories.

                              NARRATOR
It's fifty-eight. You just miss ten out when numbering them
to make it sound taller... It's almost as if you're trying
to compensate for something.

                              Beat, and then TRUMP offers the
                              box.

                              TRUMP
Would you like some chicken?

                              The NARRATOR takes a piece and
                              eyes it suspiciously.

                              NARRATOR
Has Eric touched it?

                              TRUMP
Who is Eric?

                                                    (CONTINUED)

CONTINUED:

                           TRUMP goes to sit at his desk.

                         NARRATOR
And so stands on the corner of Fifth and Fifty-Sixth stands
Trump Tower, all fifty-eight --

                         TRUMP
Sixty-eight --

                         NARRATOR
Stories high, where on one of the top floors, is taking
place a meeting of great importance that shall not be told
by I.

                           The NARRATOR exits as CONWAY
                           enters.

                         CONWAY
Mister Trump, sir.

                         TRUMP
Hello, Kellyanne Conway.

                         CONWAY
Mister Trump, I've been thinking --

                         TRUMP
No! Do not think, Kellyanne Conway. I did not make you my
campaign manager so that you could think. I made you my
campaign manager so that I could spread the illegal things
I am doing across more than one person in case Paul
Manafort ever flips. If you wanted to think, you should
have joined the campaign of Crooked Hillary Clinton.

                         CONWAY
Crooked Hillary, sir?

                         TRUMP
Yes, Crooked Hillary Clinton. I am going to call her that
from now on. I think that it is a good name for her because
she is both crooked, but she is also Hillary Clinton. It is
lucky she is called Hillary Clinton, otherwise it would not
work.

                                                  (CONTINUED)

CONTINUED:

                         CONWAY
It's --

                         TRUMP
It is. It is so great that I am actually going to go and
tweet about it right now.

                    TRUMP stands.

                         CONWAY
Mister Trump, where are you going?

                         TRUMP
My golden tweeting room, Kellyanne Conway.

                         CONWAY
Your golden tweeting room?

                         TRUMP
Let us just say that I am going to create a Republican
health care bill.

                         CONWAY
                       (nodding)
Oh, I understand.

                              TRUMP exits as CONWAY turns her
                              attention to the curtains.

                         CONWAY
                       (to herself)
What are these here for? This is an internal wall, there's
no window behind here.

                              Pulling them back, she reveals a
                              giant 6ft portrait on TRUMP and
                              attached to it, a label.

                         CONWAY
                       (reading the label)
"To Donald J. Trump. Thank you for all you do for the Trump
Foundation. From Donald J. Trump."

                                                    (CONTINUED)

>   CONWAY closes the curtains as
>   TRUMP returns.

                         TRUMP
So, where were we?

                         CONWAY
Mister Trump, as I was just saying --

>   A knock on the door interrupts.

                         TRUMP
Not now, Kellyanne Conway.
                    (shouting)
Enter.

>   A DELIVERY DRIVER enters
>   carrying food.

                         DELIVERY DRIVER
Your burger, Mister Trump.

                         TRUMP
Thank you.

>   The DELIVERY DRIVER exits.

                         CONWAY
Mister Trump, if you don't mind me asking, why are you
eating chicken if you've ordered a burger?

                         TRUMP
The chicken is a starter, I have time for one before Chris
Christie arrives. Also, I get the burger for free because I
let the local restaurant use Eric Trump as a stand-in for a
clown at a birthday party.

>   The DELIVERY DRIVER returns.

                         DELIVERY DRIVER
I'm sorry, Mister Trump. I forgot about your drink. It was
diet cola, wasn't it?

                                              (CONTINUED)

                         TRUMP
Yes. Two of them.

                         DELIVERY DRIVER
I'll go get them.

                         They exit again.

                         CONWAY
Just two? Are you cutting down?

                              The DELIVERY DRIVER returns,
                              this time carrying two large
                              barrels with "Diet Cola" written
                              on them.

                         DELIVERY DRIVER
Here you go, sir.

                         TRUMP
Thank you, delivery driver person.

                         The DELIVERY DRIVER exits.

                         TRUMP
Oh no. They did not give me a straw.

                              CHRIS CHRISTIE enters carrying a
                              deckchair.

                         CHRISTIE
Hey everyone.

                         TRUMP
Chris Christie, you just walked through a closed door.

                         CHRISTIE
Oh, did I? Jeez, I'm sorry, Mister Trump. That is new for
me. I usually manage okay with the doors, it's the bridges
that trouble me. Like that song, what is it?...

                         TRUMP
Bridge Over Troubled Water?

                                              (CONTINUED)

                    CHRISTIE
Sexy and I Know It.

                    CONWAY
Hi Chris.

                         CHRISTIE sets out his deckchair
                         and sits.

                    CHRISTIE
Hey, Kellyanne. Wow, jeez, Mister Trump, it sure is nice of
you to invite me up here. I haven't been this high since
the time was left unattended with a glue stick in the
twelfth grade.

                    TRUMP
Chris Christie, could you please come here?

                    CHRISTIE
Oh definitely. Sure thing, Mister Trump.

                         He stands and moves to TRUMP.

                    CHRISTIE
Is this what you called me here for?

                         TRUMP holds out his foot.

                    TRUMP
Yes, it is. Now kiss.

                         CHRISTIE bends down and kisses
                         TRUMP's foot.

                    TRUMP
You can leave now.

                         TRUMP returns to his chair as
                         CHRISTIE folds up his deckchair
                         and goes to leave.

                                              (CONTINUED)

                        CHRISTIE
Thank you for this opportunity, Mister Trump. I'm really
grateful for it, sir, and jeez, Mister Trump, I won't let
you down.

                CHRISTIE exits.

                        TRUMP
So, Kellyanne Conway, what was it that you were trying to
say?

                        CONWAY
I was just going to suggest that we tell Mike Pence about
everything that is going on with Russia.

                        TRUMP
That is actually a very good idea, Kellyanne Conway. Mike
Pence should know about everything going on, he is going to
need to know how Russia is helping us.

                        CONWAY
Do you want me to go talk to him right away, Mister Trump?

                        TRUMP
No. I have a much better idea. I want you to go and talk to
him right away.

                        CONWAY
Okay... I'll... go do that.

                              The DELIVERY DRIVER enters once
                              more, to hand TRUMP more food.

                        DELIVERY DRIVER
Another burger for you, Mister Trump.

                        TRUMP
Thank you.

                              The DELIVERY DRIVER exits a
                              final time.

                        TRUMP
This one is a midnight snack.

                                              (CONTINUED)

CONTINUED:

                    CONWAY
But it isn't midnight.

                    TRUMP
It is in Moscow, Kellyanne Conway. It is in Moscow.

ACT I, SCENE FOUR | PENCE & PUTIN

                              PENCE'S OFFICE, TRUMP TOWER,
                              where PENCE sits reading at his
                              desk. Opposite is a door adorned
                              with a name plaque reading
                              "Mister Mother."

                    NARRATOR
                  (entering)
And so with a job to do, Kellyanne Conway ventures upstairs
to the floor above, where sat at his desk alone is Mic,
Donald J. Trump's vice-president pick. But while she comes
to talk to Pence, yet is she to learn that talking alone is
something that only makes him tense.

                              The NARRATOR exits as CONWAY
                              enters. After knocking on the
                              door, she approaches PENCE.

                    CONWAY
Mister Pence, sir.

                              PENCE glances, then immediately
                              runs offstage.

                    CONWAY
Mister Pence?

                              CONWAY moves back through the
                              door, and PENCE returns.

                              A moment later, she tries again.

                    CONWAY
Mike...

                                            (CONTINUED)

PERFORMANCE LICENSE EDITION   LICENSE # _ _ _ _ _ _ _ _

                             PENCE runs offstage, and as
                             CONWAY moves back again, KUSHNER
                             enters.

                     CONWAY

Oh, hello, Jared.

                             KUSHNER takes a notebook and pen
                             from his pocket, writes, then
                             shows CONWAY.

                     CONWAY
                    (reading)

"Hello, Kellyanne."
                  (to KUSHNER)
Yes, hello. Look, Jared, could you help me out?

                           Again he writes then shows her.

                     CONWAY
                    (reading)
"What with?"
                  (to KUSHNER)
Well, I'm trying to talk to Mike, but he keeps running
away.

                           KUSHNER pauses then writes and
                           shows her.

                     CONWAY
                    (reading)
"Oh, don't worry about that. Mike is just scared of being
alone in the same room as a woman who isn't his wife."
                  (to KUSHNER)
Okay, so if you're not doing anything, can you come in with
me? Just so that he won't run away.

                         Again he writes then shows.

                     CONWAY
                    (reading)
"Of course, I'm not doing anything. I never do anything. I
don't serve any purpose here at all."
                  (MORE)

                            (CONTINUED)

                              CONWAY (CONT'D)
                          (to KUSHNER)
Let's go in now then.

                                        TRUMP enters behind them as
                                        PENCE returns, this time with,
                                        and in conversation with, PUTIN.

                          TRUMP
What is going on here?

                          CONWAY
Mister Trump, sir. I was trying to speak to Mike --

                          TRUMP
Who?

                          CONWAY
Mike Pence. But whenever I walk into his office he runs
away.

                          TRUMP
Okay, Kellyanne Conway. Clearly, this needs a real man, and
so I will come in with both of you.

                                        All three go through the door
                                        and approach PENCE and PUTIN.

                          CONWAY
Mister Pence, sir.

                          TRUMP
Mike Pence, and... Comrade Almighty One. What are you doing
here?

                          PUTIN
I came to fill in our Comrade about what Government of mine
are doing to help you with election win.

                          TRUMP
But how did you get in?

                          PUTIN
I have tunnel built from Trump Tower basement direct to
Kremlin. In it be fast loop.

                                                      (CONTINUED)

                         TRUMP
But those things cost billions of zillions. How did you
afford it?

                         PUTIN
I make Mexico pay for it.

                         TRUMP
That is a good idea. Kellyanne Conway, note it down, we
should use that for the wall.

                         CONWAY
So does Mike know everything now?

                         PENCE
Yes, Kellyanne. Comrade Vladimir has told me all that I
need to know.

May I also apologize for earlier. I don't feel comfortable
being in a room alone with any woman who isn't my wife. You
know how men can be.

                         CONWAY
You think there's a risk of temptation?

                         PENCE
Well, I am an old white man, Kellyanne.

                         Beat.

                         TRUMP
Hey, Comrade Vladimir Putin, did you tell Mike Pence --

                              PENCE makes a cross on his chest
                              then hits the stage with a thud.

                         PUTIN
Did I tell Mike Pence that you start worshiping me over
Jesus? No. I not tell him.

                              They all look down as KUSHNER
                              kneels to check him.

                                                      (CONTINUED)
PERFORMANCE LICENSE EDITION   LICENSE # _ _ _ _ _ _ _ _

                         TRUMP
Is he dead?

                              KUSHNER quickly writes on his
                              notepad and shows it to CONWAY.

                         CONWAY
                         (reading)
"No, he's just fainted."
                         (to all)
He's just fainted.

                         PUTIN
Donald, I leave you to clean up this mess.

                         TRUMP
Mike Pence is not a mess. Mike Pence is going to be the
reason my spirit lives on after I am impeached and
arrested.

                         PUTIN
Donald.

                         TRUMP
Sorry, Comrade Vladimir Putin, sir.

                         PUTIN
Better. Now, as I say, I leave you to clean up mess. Know
though, I never be far away... Good luck with campaign.

                              PUTIN leaves as the rest look
                              back to PENCE.

                         TRUMP
What are we going to do with Mike Pence?

                              KUSHNER writes, coughs, then
                              shows it to CONWAY.

                         CONWAY
                         (reading)
"I think we should move him."
                         (to all)
Jared Kushner thinks we should move him.

                                              (CONTINUED)

CONTINUED:

                        TRUMP

Okay. You two grab his legs, I will take his head.

                        Between them, they lift PENCE
                        and begin to carry him off.

ACT I, SCENE FIVE | THE CAMPAIGN TRAIL, PART ONE

                        Various CAMPAIGN RALLIES across
                        the country, but first, the
                        NARRATOR enters.

                        NARRATOR

And so, with the help of Russia, the campaign could not
start any lusher. But the truth remains that it's hard to
rig every state to vote for the man who wears a wig. What
he needs to get his votes is his campaign notes filled with
quotable quotes. Something to rally the crowd, something
they can go and repeat for weeks to anyone nearby by
shouting it loud. But how can he get his message across to
convince the gullible to vote him the boss? He has to
journey to the land of the normal, for rallies that are
anything but formal.

                        Lights up on the stage where
                        TRUMP stands giving a speech
                        while the ENSEMBLE (as VOTERS)
                        stand cheering. All are wearing
                        Dallas team shirts.

                        NARRATOR

Dallas, Texas.

                        TRUMP

We are going to lock her up...

                        ENSEMBLE

Lock her up! Lock her up! Lock her up!

                        TRUMP

We are going to build the wall...

                                (CONTINUED)

PERFORMANCE LICENSE EDITION   LICENSE # _ _ _ _ _ _ _ _

CONTINUED:

                          ENSEMBLE
Build the wall! Build the wall! Build the wall!

                          TRUMP
And we are going to make, this is so great, Mexico pay for
it!

                          ENSEMBLE
Who is Mexico? What is a Mexico? Where is Mexico?

                         They all remove their shirts to
                         reveal another underneath, this
                         time from a Little Rock sports
                         team.

                          NARRATOR
Little Rock, Arkansas.

                          TRUMP
Hillary Clinton is so crooked...

                          ENSEMBLE
Clinton is crooked! Clinton is crooked! Clinton is crooked!

                          TRUMP
She wants to spend money on healthcare...

                          ENSEMBLE
We're all going to die! We're all going to die! We're all
going to die!

                          TRUMP
She is such a nasty woman!

                          ENSEMBLE
What's a woman? I don't know any women! I've never touched
a woman!

                         They continue in silence,
                         changing their shirt every few
                         moments, as CONWAY and MILLER
                         enter to watch from the side.

                                                    (CONTINUED)

CONTINUED:

                    CONWAY
Why aren't there more people?

                    MILLER
I thought we were going to get thousands.

                         PUTIN enters next to them.

                    PUTIN
Do you not any idea how much it cost to convince person to
attend rally? Russia not be made of money.

                    MILLER
How come there's only one woman?

                         COHEN, wearing a torn suit,
                         enters next to them.

                    COHEN
I can only afford one.

                         The other three notice his suit.

                    MILLER
What happened to you?

                    COHEN
I can't afford a new suit. Being Trump's lawyer is
expensive.

                    CONWAY
We need more people. How can we get more?

                    MILLER
We could use children. Ivanka might lend us some of her
staff?

                    CONWAY
She pays them nearly a dollar a month. We're not paying
that much.

                                                   (CONTINUED)

                         PUTIN
I have idea.
                    (to COHEN and MILLER)
You, go.

                         Reluctantly, they follow his
                         instructions.

                         CONWAY
Do you want me to join them?

                         PUTIN
No. You stay here. We need people act as though they
support Donald convincingly.

                         The action returns to TRUMP and
                         the ENSEMBLE as they pull off
                         their final shirt and become
                         topless.

                         NARRATOR
Anchorage, Alaska.

                         TRUMP
We are going to win...

                    ENSEMBLE/ COHEN/ MILLER
We will win! We will win! We will win!

                         TRUMP
We are going to do so much winning...

                    ENSEMBLE/ COHEN/ MILLER
So much winning! So much winning! So much winning!

                         TRUMP
And now we all need to find our shirts and get out of here
before Sarah Palin turns up.

                    ENSEMBLE/ COHEN/ MILLER
No shirt! No shoes! No sophistication!

ACT I, SCENE SIX | THE RUSSIA MEETING

> TRUMP TOWER, first in the
> bedroom of TRUMP, where he sits
> in bed, wearing suit and red tie
> pajamas, trying to sleep over
> the sound of Russian music.

                    NARRATOR
                  (entering)
It's the night before the first debate, and all throughout
Trump Tower, not a single campaign ass is plotting treason
to gain power. Or so Donald thinks, for no invite has he
seen, but downstairs on the floor below, music and dancing
are the scenes.

> The NARRATOR exits.

                    TRUMP
Why can I, the great Donald J. Trump, hear music?

> The volume grows, and TRUMP
> looks around for the source,
> after a moment he checks under
> the bed.

                    TRUMP
It sounds like it is coming from below.

> He climbs out of bed and pulls
> back the cover to reveal an
> inflatable doll of himself.

                    TRUMP
You wait here for me, inflatable Donald J. Trump. I need to
go turn that music off.

> TRUMP exits as his bedroom goes
> dark, and we move to the room
> below where a party is going on.

                                                    (CONTINUED)
PERFORMANCE LICENSE EDITION   LICENSE # _ _ _ _ _ _ _

>   The music louder, JUNIOR stands
>   talking to DMITRY and PETROV
>   SUREFIRE (two Russian agents)
>   while around them half of the
>   ENSEMBLE (as RUSSIANS) are stood
>   with drinks in hand.
>
>   To the side of this main scene,
>   the other half of the ENSEMBLE
>   (as CANDIDATES) play musical
>   chairs.

                         JUNIOR
It really is no trouble for us to set this up at all,
comrades. As soon as I heard you had information on
Hillary, it was my top priority.

                         PETROV
We are here to help, Comrade.

>   They toast.

                         DMITRY
Comrades.

                         PETROV
To comrades.

                         JUNIOR
Comrades.

>   TRUMP enters and looks around
>   confused before he approaches
>   JUNIOR, who is surprised to see
>   him.

                         TRUMP
Donald Trump Junior.

                         JUNIOR
What are you doing here?

                                            (CONTINUED)

CONTINUED:

>   TRUMP
> What is going on? I thought I told you to ask before you
> invite friends over. I am trying to sleep, but all I can
> hear is your music. Do you not know that it is the first
> debate tomorrow?

>   JUNIOR
> I'm sorry, dad. But that's what these people are here for.
> They've got information on Hillary Clinton for us.

>   TRUMP
>   (pointing at the CANDIDATES)
> What about all of them? They do not look Russian.

>   JUNIOR
> Oh, they're not. They're Senate candidates. They're playing
> musical chairs to see who gets to run. When the music
> stops...

>>   There's a pause in the music,
>>   and the CANDIDATES fight for a
>>   chair until one loses and exits
>>   before the music starts again.

>   JUNIOR
> They fight. By the end of the night, we'll have just one
> person left, and they win the Senate seat. It's much
> quicker than any primary.

>   TRUMP
> But what if the public does not vote for them?

>   JUNIOR
> Russia.

>>   CONWAY enters, drink in hand,
>>   and also looking surprised.

>   CONWAY
> Mister Trump, sir. What are you doing here?

>   TRUMP
> Hello, Kellyanne Conway.

>   (CONTINUED)

                          CONWAY
                        (to JUNIOR)
I thought we weren't inviting him?

                          JUNIOR
I didn't. He just heard the music.

                          TRUMP
Why was I not supposed to be invited?

                          JUNIOR
Well, dad, you're a great guy and everything --

                    TRUMP pulls out his phone and
                    begins to type.

                          TRUMP
Continue.

                          JUNIOR
But we have to be subtle about the help we're getting, and
well, often you're not.

                          TRUMP
                    (to himself, reading)
"Just meeting with some very great people and finding out
bad stuff about Crooked Hillary Clinton. More soon." And
tweet.
                        (beat)
What was that, Donald Trump Junior?

                          JUNIOR
You know, it doesn't matter.

                    ERIC enters, a soda in hand.

                          ERIC
Hey, I'm Eric. What's your name?

                          JUNIOR
Calm down there, buddy. You don't want to be drinking too
much of that soda now, it'll upset your stomach, and you
don't want to be bringing up your alphabet pasta from
earlier, do you?

                                              (CONTINUED)
PERFORMANCE LICENSE EDITION   LICENSE # _ _ _ _ _ _ _ _

                          ERIC
But if I did, then I could eat it again for free.

                          JUNIOR
Just take it steady.

                                   ERIC moves to the side, drinks
                                   his soda in one, then begins to
                                   dance.

                          TRUMP
So tell me, what have you found out about Crooked Hillary
Clinton?

                          JUNIOR
Well, we know that she's crooked. That's a start.

                          TRUMP
Anything else?

                          JUNIOR
No. We're not sure why she is crooked, when she was
crooked, or how she was crooked.

                                   A phone rings out.

                          JUNIOR
Okay, so you know, that sounds like my phone.

                                   He takes his phone from his
                                   pocket to check it.

                          JUNIOR
I've just got a message from Julian Assange on Twitter. It
says...
                          (reading)
"I have just had my team hack the D-N-C email servers and
found this, I think it would help." And he's sent a
screenshot too. It looks as though it's an email from
Hillary to her campaign team.

                          CONWAY
What does it say?

                                                      (CONTINUED)

                         TRUMP
Can I read it, Donald Trump Junior?

                         JUNIOR
You don't know how to read, dad.

                         TRUMP

Good point. You read it then.

                         JUNIOR
                      (reading)
"Dear Subordinates. The pizzas will be delivered to the
office between six and seven P-M. Thank you for all that
you're doing."

                         TRUMP

Oh, my Comrade Putin.
                         (beat)
Wait, what does it mean?

                         JUNIOR
I think it means that she's ordered pizza.

                         TRUMP

Can we use that?

                         JUNIOR
Kellyanne, you're the campaign manager.

                         CONWAY
Well... I think it's clear. Hillary Clinton is obviously
choosing to feed her campaign team pizza over the
hardworking, patriotic American citizens of his country.

                         TRUMP
It is probably an illegal alien pizza too.

                         JUNIOR
That's it. She's feeding her campaign team Italian pizza
and taking away the jobs of American pizza. That will work,
won't it?

                         CONWAY
I think we might need something more.

                                              (CONTINUED)

CONTINUED:

                    JUNIOR
Well, we could always just edit the screenshot to make it
look like she's a trafficking people with the pizza guy?

                              TRUMP begins typing on his phone
                              again.

                    TRUMP
                 (to himself, reading)
"Just seen crooked email showing Hillary Clinton is very
crooked buying crooked pizza for her crooked team." Tweet.
                 (looking up)
Sorry, I missed that.

                    JUNIOR
Okay, so we're going with the pizza story then.

                    CONWAY
Pizza it is.

                              ERIC approaches them again.

                    ERIC
I like pizza.

                    JUNIOR
That's right, you do like pizza, buddy. But you're not
having any tonight.

                    ERIC
Hey Junior, I feel sick.

                    JUNIOR
Well, just go slow, bud. You'll be okay.

                              ERIC is sick in front of them,
                              leaving a pile of alphabet pasta
                              on the floor.

                    ERIC
Hey Junior, I was sick.

                                             (CONTINUED)

                          JUNIOR
I think it might be time for bed. Come on, I'll tuck you
in.

                              JUNIOR begins to lead ERIC
                              offstage.

                          JUNIOR
Say goodnight to everyone.

                          ERIC
Goodnight to everyone.

                              They exit.

                          CONWAY
So...

                          TRUMP
We are alone, Kellyanne Conway.

                          CONWAY
Yes. Yes, we are.

                          TRUMP
We --

                          CONWAY
So have you thought of a campaign slogan yet?

                          TRUMP
No.

                              They both look down at the
                              alphabet spaghetti.

                          CONWAY
Maybe we could get some inspiration from this?
                    (looking closer)
Look, it says M-A-W-G.

                          TRUMP
M-A-W-G? How about, make America white again?

                                              (CONTINUED)

CONTINUED:

                         CONWAY
Maybe we should go for something a little less racist.

                         TRUMP
What are you suggesting?

                              CONWAY kneels and begins to
                              rearrange letters.

                         CONWAY
Well, let's change this W with... let's see, I know, an A.
M-A-G-A.

                         TRUMP

M-A-G-A? MAGA?

                         CONWAY
Make America great again.

                              TRUMP also kneels.

                         TRUMP
I have a better idea. I am going to switch this first A
here, with this letter --

                         CONWAY
An A, Mister Trump.

                         TRUMP
Correct. M-A-G-A. Make America great again.

                              Lights out.

                         TRUMP (IN DARKNESS)
Trademark.

ACT I, SCENE SEVEN | THE FIRST DEBATE

                              HOFSTRA UNIVERSITY, LONG ISLAND,
                              where a line of light runs from
                              the front of the stage to a desk
                              set further back.

                                             (CONTINUED)

                          NARRATOR
                         (entering)
September twenty-six and the scene is set. The first
debate, an event set to be so fierce the world just can't
wait. Hofstra University on Long Island, New York, is to be
the arena, and from N-B-C, Lester Holt is to be the judge.

                              LESTER HOLT enters and addresses
                              the audience.

                          HOLT
Good evening. I'm Lester Holt.

                              He goes to sit at the desk.

                          NARRATOR
And so it comes down to Kellyanne to take on the job of
getting old Donald to budge.

                              The stage lights up to reveal to
                              podiums flanking the desk, one
                              of them being approached by
                              CONWAY pushing TRUMP.

                          TRUMP
No, Kellyanne Conway, please do not do this to me.

                          CONWAY
Come on, Mister Trump. You need to debate.

                          TRUMP
But every time I go near a black man, I say something that
makes me look bad.

                          HOLT
And in the red corner, we have... DONALD J. TRUMP!

                          TRUMP
I do not feel comfortable.

                          HOLT
And in the blue corner, we have... HILLARY RODHAM CLINTON!

                                                      (CONTINUED)

                            A CLINTON AIDE runs on stage in
                            a panic.

                        CLINTON AIDE
I don't know where she is.

                            HOLT
Do you mean to say that minutes before she's due to debate
live to the nation, Secretary Clinton still hasn't arrived?

                        CLINTON AIDE
That does appear to be the case.

                            HOLT
What's she doing? Taking the railroad here or something?

                          NARRATOR
You see, while Donald has arrived early, Hillary Clinton
will be late, or perhaps maybe, it's just that simply she
believes in fate?

                            A spotlight begins to search the
                            audience until it finds HILLARY
                            CLINTON watching from one of the
                            orchestra seats.

                          CLINTON
Oh, I'm not late. No, no, no. I've been here for hours. I'm
just watching from down here with my feet up because I'm
fairly sure I've got this one covered.

                            She turns to the person next to
                            her and pulls out her phone.

                          CLINTON
Hi, I'm Hillary Rodham Clinton, and it's nice to meet you.
I'm a relatable kind of person, as you can see. Let us take
a self-photograph together.

                            She brings her phone up but
                            quickly puts it down again.

                                           (CONTINUED)
PERFORMANCE LICENSE EDITION   LICENSE # _ _ _ _ _ _ _ _

CONTINUED:

                        CLINTON
Oh, oops. My mistake there. Just an email that I forgot to
delete. I'll just sort it.

                    She clicks on her phone.

                        CLINTON
Now you didn't see anything that you shouldn't have seen
there, did you?
                    (frightful)
Otherwise, I'm going to have to make sure I delete you too.
                    (beat, then cheerful)

Hi, I'm Hillary Rodham Clinton.

                        HOLT
Secretary Clinton, may I please ask if you've got any
intentions of joining us up here on the stage?

                        CLINTON
                    (standing)
Well, I suppose I should, Lester. I need to at least be
sporting to Donald, but I'm telling you, I'm so ready to
knock this one out of the park today.

                        CLINTON mimes a tennis shot
                        before turning to another in the
                        audience.

                        CLINTON
It's tennis.
                    (mimes again)
I play tennis. People play tennis. See? I'm a people. You
play tennis, don't you?
                    (beat, then reaches for a
                     handshake)
Nice to meet you, I'm Hillary Rodham Clinton.

                        HOLT
Madam Secretary, please can you join us so we can get his
underway?

                                            (CONTINUED)

                    CLINTON
I hear you, Lester. I'll be there in just a moment, just
have a quick matter I need to attend to first.

                              She reaches under her seat to
                              retrieve a pile of papers which
                              she hands to another in the
                              audience.

                    CLINTON
Would you mind disposing of these emails for me, please?

                              On stage, DMITRY and PETROV
                              enter and drag off the CLINTON
                              AIDE. A moment later, they
                              return with notes which they
                              begin to show TRUMP.

                    CLINTON
I'll give you a dollar for your time.

                              CLINTON pulls a dollar from her
                              pocket and hands it over.

                    CLINTON
                  (shaking hands)
Hillary Rodham Clinton. Nice to meet you.

                    HOLT
Madam Secretary.

                    CLINTON
I'm coming, Lester.

                              HOLT notices DMITRY and PETROV.

                    HOLT
Wait, Mister Trump, are you getting help from two Russians
right now?

                    TRUMP
Russians? I do not see anyone rushing. This is a debate,
Lester Holt, it is not a running race.
                    (MORE)

                                                  (CONTINUED)

CONTINUED:
                        TRUMP (CONT'D)
If it was a race, I would win, because I am athletic and I
am the best. I am a winner, everyone knows it.

                           HOLT
What the hell are you talking about?
                        (beat)
Mister Trump, there are two men standing in front of you
right this moment showing you notes.

                           TRUMP
I do not see anyone here.
                        (to PETROV and DMITRY)
What does that bit say?
                        (to HOLT)
There is no one else here, Lester Holt.
                        (to PETROV and DMITRY)
Does either of you see anyone else?

                                  DMITRY and PETROV turn to HOLT,
                                  shake their heads, then turn
                                  back to TRUMP.

                           TRUMP
Do you see that, Lester Holt? These two nice Russian men
agree with me. There is no one else here.

                           HOLT
Mister Trump, those two nice Russian men, as you put it,
are them. They just spoke.

                           TRUMP
Stop persecuting me just because of the color of my skin.
It is not my fault that I am orange. I do not deserve to be
mistreated.

                           HOLT
Mister Trump, they are stood in front of you.

                                  He stands and approaches.

                           HOLT
You are both clearly Russian agents from the Kremlin.

                                                    (CONTINUED)

CONTINUED:

                         PETROV
We're not Russian.

                         DMITRY
No. Definitely not Russian.

                         HOLT
But you're wearing the Russian flag on your shirts.

                         TRUMP
How are you speaking to ghosts, Lester Holt? I did not know
that the dead were here tonight. Steve Bannon said he was
watching from home.

                         PETROV
We're Dutch.

                         DMITRY
This is the Dutch flag.

                         HOLT
The Dutch flag goes red, white, and then blue, not white,
blue, and then red.

                         DMITRY
It's the alternative Dutch flag.

                                   CLINTON finally makes it to the
                                   stage.

                         CLINTON
I'm here, Lester. You can stop all your worrying now.

                                   HOLT turns to her as the DMITRY
                                   and PETROV exit quickly.

                         HOLT
Finally.

                                   He turns back to TRUMP.

                         HOLT
Wait, where have the Russians gone?

                                                      (CONTINUED)

PERFORMANCE LICENSE EDITION   LICENSE # _ _ _ _ _ _ _ _

                         TRUMP
There were no Russians. They were ghosts.

                         HOLT
Mister Trump, what are you talking about?

                         TRUMP
Woooooo. Wooooooooo. Wooooooooooo.
                    (beat)
Woo.

                         Shaking his head, HOLT returns
                         to his desk.

                         HOLT
Let's just get this over with.

                         CLINTON approaches the NARRATOR
                         to shake hands.

                         CLINTON
Hi. I'm Hillary Rodham Clinton, nice to meet you.

                         NARRATOR
Narrator.

                         CLINTON
Nice to meet you, Nar-ray-tor.

                         She laughs to herself.

                         NARRATOR
                    (forced)
Ha.

                         CLINTON
Did you see that? Did everyone see that? I made a joke, and
you laughed because it was a funny joke. Jokes are funny,
and jokes are relatable.
                    (beat)
I'm Hillary Rodham Clinton. I'm here for the next eight
years.
                         (MORE)

                                                   (CONTINUED)

CONTINUED:

                          CLINTON (CONT'D)
                    (putting her arm around the
                     NARRATOR)
You know, I think we're going to be the best of friends.

                          HOLT
Secretary Clinton, for the last time --

                          CLINTON
I'm taking my place, Lester. Keep your hair on, or you'll
end up looking like Donald.

                          HOLT
Touché.

                          CLINTON
Exactly, Lester.

                              CLINTON takes her place at her
                              podium as the NARRATOR goes to
                              kneel next to HOLT.

                          HOLT
                    (clears throat)
Hello, and welcome to the first Presidential debate of the
two thousand and sixteen election. I will be your moderator
for tonight's increasingly personal argument, Lester Holt.

                          CLINTON
Hi, Lester. I'm Hillary Rodham Clinton.

                          HOLT
Madam Secretary, I know who you are.

                          TRUMP
And I am...

                          HOLT
Mister Trump?

                          TRUMP
Hold on, Lester Holt.

                              He takes a drawing from his
                              pocket and unfolds it.

                                              (CONTINUED)

                         TRUMP
                       (reading)
"I am Eric."

                         HOLT
I'm sorry?

                         TRUMP
No, you are Lester Holt.

                         HOLT
Mister Trump, you're not Eric.

                         TRUMP
I was reading from a good luck picture that my son drew for
me.

                    He shows off the drawing.

                         TRUMP
He drew a bunny.

                         HOLT
Can we please just start this debate?

                         CLINTON
Of course, Lester. Let's get on with it.

                         HOLT
Thank you.
                       (beat)
And so onto this evening's first topic, achieving
prosperity. Secretary Clinton, you have the floor.

                         TRUMP
Does that mean I have the roof?

                         CLINTON
Thank you, Lester. I have a very clear position on this
subject. I think that for America to achieve prosperity and
be successful, we need to be investing in education.

                    She mimes a tennis shot.

                                              (CONTINUED)

                         TRUMP
I think that too, but I thought of it first. Clearly,
Crooked Hillary Clinton is just stealing my ideas on
controlling immigration.

                         HOLT
Mister Trump, this section isn't about controlling
immigration, it's about achieving prosperity.

                         TRUMP
Are they not the same thing?

                         HOLT
No, Mister Trump, they are not the same thing.

                              The NARRATOR raises their arm on
                              CLINTON's side.

                         NARRATOR
Fifteen-love.

                         HOLT
Madam Secretary, would you like to continue?

                         CLINTON
Certainly, Lester. So, you know, today happens to be my
little granddaughters second birthday. She's a sweet, small
and polite girl, although that will soon change when she
starts kindergarten, but it means that I know first hand
just how important it is to ensure we're able to offer a
high level of quality education to everyone from a young
age.

                              She mimes another tennis shot.

                         HOLT
Mister Trump, your response, please.

                         TRUMP
Well, I too know just how important education, and also one
million dollars from your father, is at a young age.

                         (MORE)

                                             (CONTINUED)

CONTINUED:

> ### TRUMP (CONT'D)
> Not a lot of people know this, but I have a son, and his name is Eric Trump, and he is still in kindergarten, but soon, when we have worked out how to teach him potty, he will be starting big boy school.

>> Beat, then the NARRATOR holds up their arm again.

> ### NARRATOR
> Thirty-love.

> ### HOLT
> Secretary Clinton.

> ### CLINTON
> Oh, is it my turn again already? How exciting, I'm enjoying this. Well, let me go on by telling you exactly how I will help this to bring prosperity back to this country... I will not do anything that Donald Trump would do.

>> She mimes another tennis shot.

> ### TRUMP
> What people need to know about this woman is that she is a very crooked woman. Crooked Hillary Clinton. No one has ever been more crooked than Hillary Clinton. I do not know why or when she was crooked, but I have just here, in my pocket --

> ### HOLT
> Mister Trump?

>> TRUMP pulls out another drawing.

> ### TRUMP
> I have here an email that Hillary Clinton sent to someone on her campaign team, and it says, just here that... Oh, no, this is just another picture Eric Trump drew for me.

>> He shows off the drawing of a cat.

> ### TRUMP
> He drew a dog. Look, you can see its whiskers.

(CONTINUED)

                         HOLT
Mister Trump, what is this email that you are on about?

                              TRUMP reaches under his podium
                              to pick up a giant tennis ball.

                         TRUMP
It is an email that Crooked Hillary Clinton sent to
someone, and it proves that she is a very bad and also a
very crooked person who orders crooked pizza for her
crooked team. It was sent to my campaign by a great man
called Julian Assange, who does great things, and he and
WikiLeaks, with the help of Russia, hacked her email.

                         HOLT
Wait, you're saying that Russia and WikiLeaks hacked
Secretary Clinton's email, and all they found was that she
ordered pizza?

                         TRUMP
Did I mention that it was a crooked pizza?

                              He attempts to throw the tennis
                              ball, but it bounces back at
                              him.

                              DMITRY and PETROV return to talk
                              to TRUMP.

                         HOLT
So now the Russians are back.

                              CLINTON exits the returns a
                              moment later with an automatic
                              tennis ball launcher as the
                              DMITRY and PETROV leave again.

                         TRUMP
They were not Russians, Lester Holt. I would also to change
what I just said. I do not have an email, I did not get it
from Julian Assange, he did not get it from WikiLeaks, and
they did not get help from Russia to hack the D-N-C. None
of that happened, so bless Comrade Vladimir Putin.

                                              (CONTINUED)

                              HOLT
That is an incredibly specific statement for you to make,
Mister Trump.

                              TRUMP
Wrong.

                              HOLT
Secretary Clinton, back to you.

                              CLINTON
Oh, yes, thank you, Lester. Well, you may have all seen
there how Donald attempted to distract everyone from his
misdeeds. Speaking of which, I'm wondering just how many of
them he's going to be bringing up tonight. Perhaps he might
mention his fake university that has been scamming the
vulnerable out of thousands of dollars?

                                        She taps the top of the
                                        launcher, and it fires a ball
                                        towards TRUMP.

                              CLINTON
Or perhaps the time he was sued for refusing to rent out
his properties to minority communities because he is a
racist?
                              (another tap)
Or the numerous businesses he's caused the failure or
bankruptcy of? Trump Steaks.
                              (another tap)
Trump Vodka.
                              (another tap)
Trump Atlantic City.
                              (another tap)
Numerous Trump golf courses.
                              (multiple taps)
Trump Airlines.
                              (another tap)
Trump Ice.
                              (another tap)
The year two thousand Trump Presidential Election campaign.
                              (another tap)
And, of course, his greatest failure of all, Eric Trump.
                              (a final tap)

                                                    (CONTINUED)

PERFORMANCE LICENSE EDITION   LICENSE # _ _ _ _ _ _ _ _

CONTINUED:

                         TRUMP
Wrong. That is just not fair. A lot of that is true, but I
cannot take responsibility for that kid. Have you actually
seen him? That level of stupidity only comes naturally.

                         HOLT
Is there anything else that you'd like to add, Secretary
Clinton?

                         CLINTON
No, I'm done, Lester.

                         HOLT
Okay, Mister --

                         CLINTON
Wait, I've remembered! Trumped-up trickle-down economics.

                              She opens her mouth, and
                              theatrical flames shoot across
                              the stage.

                         HOLT
You know, Mister Trump? You shouldn't have moved out the
way. You could have had eyes that match the rest of your
face.

                              CONWAY enters, burnt, and with a
                              tennis ball in her mouth. She
                              spits it out then exits.

                         HOLT
So, Mister Trump, would you like to respond at all?

                         TRUMP
                        (quietly)
My microphone is not working, Lester Holt. I did not hear
what she said.

                         HOLT
I'm sorry, Mister Trump, what was that? I couldn't hear
you.

                                             (CONTINUED)

                         TRUMP
                      (shouting)
I said that my microphone is not working, and because of
it, I could not hear what Crooked Hillary Clinton said.

                         HOLT
Okay, firstly, Mister Trump, it's clear to all of us that
you were just whispering. And, secondly, you don't listen
with a microphone.

                         TRUMP
Do you not?

                         HOLT
No, Mister Trump. You do not.

                         TRUMP
                      (quietly)
It is broken again.

                         HOLT
I'm sorry?

                         TRUMP
                      (shouting)
I said that it is broken again.

                         HOLT
Clearly, Mister Trump, it is not broken.

                         CLINTON
It's okay, Lester. I can fix it.

                              CLINTON walks over to TRUMP and
                              adjusts his microphone.

                         TRUMP
Thank you, Crooked Hillary Clinton.

                         CLINTON
Don't mention it, Donald.
                    (pointing suddenly up)
What's that up there?

                                              (CONTINUED)

                         TRUMP
Where?
                         (begins pointing)
I do not see anything.

                         CLINTON
                    (pointing down)
And down there.

                              TRUMP begins to point down with
                              his other hand as though in a
                              dance pose.

                         CLINTON
Just hold that for a moment.

                              She pulls out her phone, steps
                              back, and takes a photo.

                         CLINTON
Got it.

                              CLINTON hands her phone to the
                              NARRATOR.

                         CLINTON
Would you mind sending that photo to the media for me? I'd
do it myself, but I'm not too good with emails.

                         NARRATOR
Okay.

                         CLINTON
Thanks. I'm Hillary Rodham Clinton, nice to meet you again.

                              She returns to her podium as the
                              NARRATOR lifts their arm again.

                         NARRATOR
Forty-love. Matchpoint.

                         HOLT
Can we get back to debating now?

                                                   (CONTINUED)

                        TRUMP

MAGA!

                        HOLT

What's MAGA?

                        TRUMP

Thank you, Lester Holt, for asking me about MAGA. MAGA is
MAGA.

                        HOLT

Yes, I got that bit.

                        TRUMP

It stands for Make America great again, and I am very glad
that you like it, Lester Holt.

                        HOLT

Wait a moment, I never said that I like it, Mister Trump.

                        TRUMP

MAGA!

                        HOLT

I'm sorry?

                        TRUMP

MAGA! MAGA!

                        HOLT

Secretary Clinton, do you have anything to say?

                        CLINTON

Yes, I do. On education --

                        TRUMP

MAGA!

                        CLINTON

Healthcare --

                        TRUMP

MAGA! MAGA!

                                               (CONTINUED)

CONTINUED:

                         CLINTON
National security --

                         TRUMP
MAGA! MAGA! MAGA!

                         CLINTON
The economy --

                         TRUMP
MAGA! MAGA! MAGA! MAGA!

                         CLINTON
Immigration --

                         TRUMP
Deport the children.

                         CLINTON
Infrastructure --

                         TRUMP
MAGA! MAGA! MAGA! MAGA! MAGA!

                         HOLT falls from his chair onto
                         the floor. The NARRATOR helps
                         him up, but he now has visibly
                         white hair.

                         HOLT
                   (exhausted)
That's --

                         TRUMP
MAGA!

                         HOLT
Time.

                         TRUMP approaches HOLT.

                         TRUMP
Lester Holt --

                                                    (CONTINUED)

CONTINUED:

> CONWAY enters and with the
> NARRATOR'S help, drags him
> offstage.
>
> CLINTON approaches HOLT as he
> recomposes himself.

                    CLINTON
Good debate, hey Lester? Any chance of a friendly chat with
you?

                    HOLT
Oh, I would love to Secretary Clinton, but I'm already late
for my... Mongolian cookery class.

                    CLINTON
Well, okay then.
                    (to audience)
Hey everyone, I'm Hillary Rodham Clinton, and I'm going to
be your president.

> Happy with herself, she exits
> while performing a unique dance.

ACT I, SCENE EIGHT | THE VICE-PRESIDENTIAL DEBATE

> LONGWOOD UNIVERSITY, FARMVILLE,
> and the NARRATOR enters a
> spotlight.

                    NARRATOR
And so with the first debate over the campaigns rage strong
with the anticipation for the second high, but the wait not
too long. But first, we journey to Longwood University in
Farmville, Virginia, for it's October fourth and the
running mates have opinions of their own to set forth.

> TIM KAINE and PENCE enter from
> opposite wings to flank the
> NARRATOR.

                    KAINE
Hello. I'm Tim Kaine.

                                        (CONTINUED)

                         PENCE
And I'm Mike Pence. Hello.

                         NARRATOR
But no one really cared about their debate so we'll just
move on.

                         PENCE
Goodbye.

                         KAINE
Well, bye now.

                    KAINE and PENCE exit.

ACT I, SCENE NINE | THE CAMPAIGN TRAIL, PART TWO

                              VARIOUS SETTINGS, but first the
                              AMERICAN MIDWEST where CLINTON
                              stands talking to a MIDWESTERN
                              VOTER.

                         NARRATOR
And so to the trail we do return, where we join our friend
Hillary still failing to learn. For in the Midwest, she's
trying to relate to a voter, Bill Clinton with her to help
try promote her.

                         CLINTON
Hi, I'm Hillary Rodham Clinton.

                         MIDWESTERN VOTER
Screw you, Hillary. Your husband cost me my job.

                    BILL CLINTON enters.

                         BILL
Can I help here, Hillary?

                         CLINTON
Go away, Bill.

                                        (CONTINUED)

CONTINUED:

                          BILL
Okay, I'm going.

                                        BILL, CLINTON, and the
                                        MIDWESTERN VOTER exit.

                                        CONWAY (in disguise), MILLER,
                                        TRUMP, and the ENSEMBLE (as
                                        VOTERS) enter.

                          NARRATOR
But it was not only for Clinton that things were going
wrong, for over on the East Coast, team Trump are also not
so strong. For now, we join them in Boston, where their
campaign manager stands in costume.

                          TRUMP
Hello Boston.

                          ENSEMBLE
BOO!

                          TRUMP
That is a Giuliani approval.

                          MILLER
Kellyanne, why are you wearing that disguise?

                          CONWAY
Oh, this? It's because some people in Massachusetts still
want to stick me on a dunk tank to see if I'll float.

ACT I, SCENE TEN | THE SECOND DEBATE

                                        WASHINGTON UNIVERSITY, ST. LOUIS
                                        where ANDERSON COOPER and MARTHA
                                        RADDATZ sit at a desk flanked on
                                        both sides by the ENSEMBLE (as
                                        VOTERS). Among them, DMITRY,
                                        ERIC, JUNIOR, and KUSHNER, all
                                        in disguise.

                                                            (CONTINUED)

                         NARRATOR
                       (entering)
And so we reach our second debate, a further ninety minutes
for the candidates to share the hate. But this second is to
be different from the first, and not only because it's
going to be the worst. This is the time to hear the views
of all, and so this debate is to be a town hall. Questions
asked by the undecided to earn every vote, questions
designed to gain answers that are only of note. Questions
like, how can so many people still be undecided?
                       (beat)
From C-N-N and A-B-C are our moderators for the night,
Anderson Cooper, and Martha Raddatz.

                         RADDATZ
Good evening.

                         COOPER
Hello.

                         NARRATOR
And so with the stage all set, all that's left --

                    The NARRATOR is interrupted by
                    COOPER beginning to laugh.

                         RADDATZ
Anderson, are you okay?

                         COOPER
It's just so stupid.

                         RADDATZ
Anderson?

                         COOPER
                       (laughing harder)
Why are we here?

                         RADDATZ
We're moderating the debate.

                                              (CONTINUED)

                         COOPER
But why are we debating? It's so stupid to think that
Donald Trump actually has a chance.

                         RADDATZ
Pull yourself together. This is a presidential debate, the
world is watching us.

                              COOPER sighs then composes
                              himself.

                         COOPER
                    (to the NARRATOR)
Continue, please.

                         NARRATOR
And so with the stage all set, all that's left is to
introduce the candidates.

                         The NARRATOR exits.

                         RADDATZ
Are you okay now?

                         COOPER
I think so.

                         RADDATZ
Okay, let's do this.

                         Beat.

                         COOPER
Good evening, I'm Anderson Cooper.

                         RADDATZ
I'm Martha Raddatz.

                         COOPER
This is the second presidential debate.

                         RADDATZ
And it's time to meet the candidates. First up, it's
Hillary Rodham Clinton.

                                             (CONTINUED)

                              CLINTON enters, waves to the
                              audience, then takes the stool
                              that waits for her.

                        COOPER
And up against her, it's sexual offender --

                        RADDATZ coughs.

                        COOPER
Alleged sexual offender, Donald J. Trump.

                              TRUMP enters and confused,
                              circles his stool for a moment
                              before sitting.

                     RADDATZ
Good evening to you both.

                     CLINTON
Good evening subjects.

                      TRUMP
Yes, I think that I am the perfect role model for all young
people in America. Why would the young boys not want to all
grow up to be just like me, the great Donald J. Trump? I
can do whatever I want. I have money, I have a tower, I
have a plane, I used to have a TV show, and I can even brag
about assaulting women on camera and still be considered
for the presidency.

                      Beat.

                     COOPER
Okay, Mister Trump... Well, we're going to get started with
our first question of the night now, which comes from John
Johnson.

                     JUNIOR stands.

                                                (CONTINUED)

                          JUNIOR
Good evening, I am John Johnson. My question is, do the
candidates think that they are a good role model for young
people in this country? Especially young boys, who, as we
all know, are the real future.

                     ERIC applauds.

                          ERIC
Go, Junior!

                         RADDATZ
Mister Trump, would you like to answer first?

                          TRUMP
I have already answered. Did you not hear my answer? I
answered just before he asked the question.

                         RADDATZ
                      (suspiciously)
Yes, Mister Trump, we noticed that.

                         COOPER
Let's move on to your answer then, Secretary Clinton.

                         CLINTON
Well obviously, of course, I think that I am a good role
model for young people. How could the country's first
female nominee of a major party and soon to be the first
women as president, not be a good role model? I do think
it's important to say though, all young people deserve a
role model, the young girls just as much as the young boys.

                          TRUMP
Well, I actually agree with all of that, except for all of
the bits that I do not agree with. I do not think that it
is important for you girls to have a role model. All that
young girls need to know is that they should marry rich.

                         COOPER
My god, Mister Trump.

                                              (CONTINUED)

                        TRUMP
No, Anderson Cooper, I am not your god. God lives, as we
all know, in a big red castle in Moscow.

                        COOPER
Secretary Clinton, do you have a response?

                        CLINTON
Oh, I... did he really just say that?

                        COOPER
I think he did, yes.

                        TRUMP
You hear me correctly, Crooked Hillary Clinton. I would
also like to add...

                              He pulls out notes and checks
                              them.

                        TRUMP
I think that it is very unfair that rich people should ever
have to pay for the healthcare of the poor. I worked very
hard to scam my way to becoming a fake billionaire.

                        RADDATZ
Mister Trump, I'm not sure what you were answering there,
so we're going to move onto our second question.

                        COOPER
Which tonight comes from a mister V ordinary American
voter. Mister American voter, what is your question?

                              DMITRY stands.

                        DMITRY
Yes, hello. I am ordinary American voter boy who likes
American things like baseball and cheese that not be made
of cheese. I am fourteen years of age.

                        RADDATZ
And what is your question?

                                                    (CONTINUED)

                         DMITRY
My question is for Mister Donald Trump, do you think that
it is unfair for rich people to ever be expected to pay for
the healthcare of the poor?

                         RADDATZ
Mister Trump, didn't you also just answer that question
before it was asked too?

                         TRUMP
Yes, I did, Martha Raddatz. It is a great question, and I
gave a great answer.

                         RADDATZ
Okay, is there something going on here?

                         COOPER
Martha --

                         RADDATZ
                    (ignoring COOPER)
It's almost as though you've been colluding with the people
here tonight so that you can find out the questions before
we began.

                         COOPER
Please consider what you're actually accusing the Trump
campaign of.

                         RADDATZ
You're right, Anderson, none of them have the intelligence
to plan that.

                         COOPER
Let's just move onto the next question.

                         CLINTON
Oh, don't I get to say anything?

                         COOPER
You wanted to say something inspiring about how you've got
a plan to solve all the issues surrounding healthcare in
this country, Secretary Clinton?

                                              (CONTINUED)

CONTINUED:

                         CLINTON
No, I'll pass.

                         COOPER
We'll move on then.

                         RADDATZ
Our third question tonight comes from Mister Eric.

                    ERIC stands.

                         ERIC
Hey, I'm Eric.

                         RADDATZ
And what is your question, Mister Eric?

                         ERIC
I forgot.

                         DMITRY
                    (to JUNIOR)
Why did we have to bring him again?

                         JUNIOR
I had no choice but to bring him along. His wife said she
wanted a night off.

                         RADDATZ
Well, I guess if we haven't got a question, then we have no
choice but to move on.

                         COOPER
And it's our final question of the night which comes from
John Johnson Junior.

                         DMITRY
                    (to KUSHNER)
Could you not think of anything more original?

                         TRUMP
I like this question.

                                                  (CONTINUED)

                              KUSHNER stands with a number of
                              cue cards.

                    COOPER
              (reading)
"John Johnson Junior."
              (KUSHNER drops a card)
"My question is."
              (KUSHNER drops a card)
"Hello, my name is."
              (KUSHNER drops a card)
"It's nice to be here."
              (KUSHNER drops a card)
"Crooked Hillary Clinton is Crooked."
              (KUSHNER drops a card)
"But, what are you going."
              (KUSHNER drops a card)
"We all know that."
              (KUSHNER drops a card)
"To do about it?"

                    Beat.

                    COOPER
I think that you might have your cue cards in the wrong
order, Mister Johnson Junior.

                    DMITRY
I think what my friend is trying to ask here is what is
Mister Trump going to do about Hillary Clinton being
crooked?
              (to KUSHNER)
Is that not correct?

                    KUSHNER nods.

                    DMITRY
              (to COOPER)
You see?

                    RADDATZ
Okay, I'm sorry, but there is definitely something strange
going on here.

                                        (CONTINUED)

                              COOPER
I have to agree. The punctuation on those cue cards is
terrible.

                              CLINTON
You know, Anderson, I think Martha has a point. Donald has
clearly found out what the questions will be before the
debate, and I would go so far as to say he chose a few of
them too.

                              COOPER
That is a serious allegation, Secretary Clinton, but I can
see your point.

                              RADDATZ
There's certainly circumstantial evidence.

                              COOPER
Quite right.
                          (to CLINTON)
Well, we could stop this debate, choose new voters with new
questions, and start again. Would you like us to do that,
Secretary Clinton?

                              CLINTON
I think that is the only --

                              COOPER
I would also like to take this chance to remind you that
you're ahead in all polls and there is a free minibar in
your hotel room.

                              CLINTON
I think we can just let Donald answer this question.

                              COOPER
Mister Trump, your answer.

                              TRUMP
I am going to lock her up.

                              RADDATZ
Is that it?

                                                    (CONTINUED)

                         TRUMP
My supporters cannot remember more than three words at one
time.

                         COOPER
And with that, we have reached the end of our questions for
tonight's debate. Before we finish, though, while this is
not customary for a moderator, there is one subject that I
would like to bring up myself. Mister Trump, as I'm sure
you're aware, a few days ago, footage was leaked of you
bragging about sexually assaulting a woman.

                         RADDATZ
Yes, thank you for mentioning it, Anderson. I would like to
ask some questions about that tape if you don't mind. What
were you thinking? And do you not have even the smallest
amount of respect for women?

                         TRUMP
Firstly, it was just locker room talk, nothing more. And
secondly, correct.

                         RADDATZ
I think that a lot of people across the country would have
found it difficult to watch that footage or read about the
comments you made, and in some cases, I am sure that it
would have brought back memories of events some women would
rather forget. Do you not feel any remorse at all, Mister
Trump?

                         TRUMP
No, next question.

                         RADDATZ
Well, I think that the comments you made on that tape are
truly disgusting, Mister Trump. I've got to say it.

                         TRUMP
Thank you. But I do not think that you can have a fair
opinion because you are clearly biased. Not only are you a
woman, but you are also only a six out of ten.

                                                       (CONTINUED)

CONTINUED:

                          COOPER
Mister Trump, I am not a woman, and I also think that what
you said was disgusting.

                          TRUMP
Well, that is because you look like a little old lady.

                          CLINTON
Anderson, if I could comment?

                          COOPER
Go ahead, Secretary Clinton.

                          CLINTON
I, like a lot of people, watched the footage of Donald that
was leaked earlier this week with a feeling of sickness in
my stomach. At one point, I did, in fact, feel so sick that
I thought I was going to be, but thankfully I was able to
wash it all down with a bottle of champagne.

                          RADDATZ
Mister Trump, is there anything at all that you would like
to say in response to Secretary Clinton or the leaking of
this tape?

                          TRUMP
Yes, I would like to say, live from New York --

                          COOPER
Wrong show, Mister Trump. Your response, please.

                          TRUMP
                    (pointing into the audience)
What is that?

                                   As they all turn to look where
                                   he's pointing, TRUMP makes a run
                                   for it and exits.

                          COOPER
I don't see anything, Mister --

                          RADDATZ
Where did he go?

                                                      (CONTINUED)

                        CLINTON
I didn't see anything.

                        RADDATZ
Well, if he's not here, then we can't really carry on, so
we're going to have to wrap up this debate and declare
Hillary Clinton winner by default.

                        COOPER
Our thanks to Secretary Clinton this evening and to all of
you for watching. I've been Anderson Cooper.

                        RADDATZ
I've been Martha Raddatz.

                        COOPER
And this has been the second presidential debate. Goodnight
to you all.

                        RADDATZ
Goodnight.

                              Beat, and then CLINTON walks
                              over to them.

                        CLINTON
Hey, Anderson, Martha --

                        COOPER
I would love to stay and catch up, Secretary Clinton, but I
have my... cross country skiing lesson to attend.

                        RADDATZ
And I said I'd give him a lift.

                              COOPER and RADDATZ exit in a
                              hurry.

                        CLINTON
Oh, well, okay then. Maybe next time.

ACT I, SCENE ELEVEN | THE ENDORSEMENTS

>   NO SPECIFIC SETTING, but the
>   NARRATOR stands center stage.

NARRATOR

And so with two debates down and just one to go, the war
rages stronger than ever, and the opinion of both sides
that the other could win? Never.

But just as in any battle, there are secret weapons known
to very few, or at least on team Trump, that is certainly
true. For there are statements of endorsements from the
famous kind, and for Clinton, they came in their hundreds,
while from Trump how there was any, one only wonders.

>   Inspiring sounding music begins
>   to play.

NARRATOR

And on team Clinton, we have...

>   As the NARRATOR exits, a
>   spotlight finds BILL.

BILL

This election day, I'm endorsing my wife, Hillary Clinton.
                    (beat)
Hillary, can I have my medication back now?

>   This time the spotlight finds
>   BARACK OBAMA and MICHELLE OBAMA.

OBAMA

Well, hello to all of you... Barack Obama here, that's
President Barack Obama... I'm here today with my lovely
wife Michelle, who I love very much... and who I am married
to, we also have two beautiful children... we're a family.

                                              (CONTINUED)

MICHELLE

We just wanted to take the time to visit this theatrical
venue for the creative arts, something that both me and
Barack view as such a vital part of everyday life and a
place where families like ours come together for
enlightenment and entertainment brought to us by the very
talented performers on the stage, to endorse for the forty-
fifth Presidency of these United States --

OBAMA

That is the forty-fifth since our founding father George
Washington was our first.

MICHELLE

Both mine and Barack's good friend, Hillary Rodham Clinton.

OBAMA

Because we're stronger... together.
                    (beat, then to MICHELLE)
That should stop her from calling us every night.

                              Moving again, the spotlight
                              finds BERNIE SANDERS.

SANDERS

A recount, I would like to request a recount. What? I was
told this was the line to request recounts. The Hillary
Clinton endorsement line? No, no. That would be like your
flight being thirty minutes late and then going and writing
the airline a five-star review on Yelp. I want to request a
recount.

                              This time, it finds JOHN OLIVER.

OLIVER

Well, hello and welcome, America. There's just time for a
quick round-up of this shit show so far, and well basically
America, here we are, we're either screwed, or we're
slightly less screwed.

                         (MORE)

                                                    (CONTINUED)

CONTINUED:

                           OLIVER (CONT'D)
I'm British, and so it would be wrong of me to make any
endorsement right now, but please, America, we've been
through a lot together, don't mess it up now by this
bargain-basement liberty torching day of democracy fiddling
voting for Donald Trump. The man looks like a baboon's anus
experiencing difficulties after the baboon ate a
particularly large tangerine. **Bad baboon, don't eat that
particularly large tangerine, baboon.**
                    (beat)
And now, this...

                                        The music changes to that of a
                                        comical nature as the spotlight
                                        finds MIKE HUCKABEE.

                           HUCKABEE
Did y'all hear the one about the chicken crossin' the road?
It was running away from Hillary Clinton folks. Well
anyway, vote Donal' Trump, 'cause at least he comes with a
penis.

                                        This time, it finds SARAH PALIN.

                           PALIN
Well, I gotta' say, it sure is nice of you all to silence
the applause quickly so you can hear my thoughts on a few
matters. You know, usually, to speak to an audience this
big I have to run into a town hall meeting and scream help,
there's a polar bear chasing me.

                           NARRATOR
Are you okay, Sarah?

                           PALIN
Oh, me? I'm fine. It's sweet of you to ask, though. It's
pretty sweet to be here too. Who would have thought that I
would ever be relevant again?
                    (laughs to herself)
I thought about it for a while, though. I said to myself,
Sarah, you've been relevant before and it could come back,
you know. Well, I guess you're all thinking I'm not so bad
right now, aren't you? --

                                                  (CONTINUED)

                         NARRATOR
                        (coughing)
Sarah, if you could, please get on with it.

                         PALIN
Oh right. I'm sorry. Sometimes I just let myself get
carried away, and it's like, Sarah, what are you doing?
Anyway, I'd like to endorse the white guy.

                         NARRATOR

Thank you.

                         PALIN
Oh, can I say something else? I was really hoping I could
plug my Soundcloud while I'm here. On it, you can find all
of your favorite gay anthems but rewritten for us good old
law-abiding religious folk who think the only thing that
should go near a vagina is a penis and vacuum cleaner once
a month to tidy it all up real good for date night. As a
special bonus, if you go there now, you'll also find Palin
does the Village People, featuring Trey Gowdy as the cowboy
and Mike Pence as the police officer. I'm the construction
worker.

                              Moving for a final time, the
                              spotlight finds TRUMP wearing
                              glasses.

                         TRUMP
I am David Dennison, and I am an ordinary American voter
from the state of East Dakota. I would like to endorse the
very great, trust me, no one is greater, Donald J. Trump,
to make America great again.

ACT I, SCENE TWELVE | THE THIRD DEBATE

                              The UNIVERSITY OF NEVADA, LAS
                              VEGAS, where the NARRATOR stands
                              front center while behind them,
                              CLINTON and TRUMP stand at
                              podiums opposite sides of CHRIS
                              WALLACE who sits at a desk.

                                                  (CONTINUED)

                          NARRATOR
And so we reach our third debate, the final, the last, the
one to decide the world's fate. Fox News is this time to
host, the channel which we feel we can joke the most...
only we're not sure they've got a sense of humor, and we
don't want to be sued.

                    The NARRATOR exits.

                          WALLACE
Good evening to you all and welcome to the third
presidential debate. That's right, third because apparently
this election hasn't been embarrassing enough yet. I will
be your moderator for this evening, Chris Wallace. Now,
let's meet our candidates, and first up it's --

                          CLINTON
President Hillary Clinton.

                          WALLACE
I'm sorry, Secretary Clinton?

                          CLINTON
President Hillary Clinton, nice to meet you.

                          WALLACE
President? You do know that the election isn't until next
week?

                          CLINTON
Yes, I do know that, Chris. But I think that I'm going to
be okay. I've already had President Clinton printed on
those little pens they give out to visitors to the White
House. Bill had some left, but I wanted new ones that write
in red ink, it's the color of blood.

                          WALLACE
That is an awful lot of confidence you've got, Secretary
Clinton.

                          CLINTON
Well, Chris, I can have that level of confidence. I mean,
it's not like someone, let us say, F-B-I director, James
Comey, is going to murder my campaign.
                          (MORE)
                                              (CONTINUED)
PERFORMANCE LICENSE EDITION   LICENSE # _ _ _ _ _ _ _ _

CONTINUED:

                    CLINTON (CONT'D)
No one would be that desperate for attention that they'd
risk all of our democracy and nuclear war. Knocking on
wood, of course.

                         CLINTON taps the top of her
                         podium.

                    WALLACE
Secretary Clinton, I believe those podiums are actually
made from imitation wood.

                    CLINTON
Well, gosh dang.

                         Beat.

                    WALLACE
Okay, well, can everyone please give a hand to our first
candidate, Secretary Hillary Clinton.

                    CLINTON
Nice to meet you all.

                    WALLACE
And now, please give the finger to our second candidate,
Donald J. Trump.

                    TRUMP
Does anyone know how long this will be? Only, I have left
Eric Trump in the parking lot, and I forgot to open a
window.

                    WALLACE
The debate is ninety minutes, Mister Trump, but let's not
waste any time as we move to the first question. Mister
Trump, what is your opinion on birth control?

                    TRUMP
I like birth control. I mean, look at me, no one likes
birth control more than I do. I am a walking advertisement
for birth control.

                    WALLACE
Secretary Clinton, the same question to you.

                                              (CONTINUED)

                         CLINTON
Well, I am quite clear on this subject. I believe that all
women should have access to birth control at no cost and
without the judgment or interference of anyone else,
especially men. Why do I think this? I'm simply just not an
asshole --

                         TRUMP
Wrong.

                         WALLACE
I'm sorry, what was that, Mister Trump? You think that
Secretary Clinton is an asshole?

                         CLINTON
It's okay, Chris. It takes one to know one, and Donald
certainly is one.

                         WALLACE
Okay, we'll move on to another question now, this time for
you, Secretary Clinton.

                         CLINTON
Ask away, Chris. Anything you like, I'm happy to give you a
clear answer.

                         WALLACE
Thank you. About your emails…

                         Beat.

                         CLINTON
I would like to retract my previous statement.

                         WALLACE
Secretary Clinton, I'm sure that you're aware by now that
there are a lot of questions being raised about your emails
in the past week.

                         CLINTON
Yes, well about those...

                              CLINTON makes her way into the
                              audience.

                                              (CONTINUED)

CONTINUED:

                         WALLACE
Secretary Clinton, where are you going?

                         CLINTON
I won't be a moment, Chris.

                         WALLACE
Please don't leave me alone with Donald.

                                   CLINTON approaches the audience
                                   member who she gave her earlier
                                   emails to.

                         CLINTON
I thought I told you to destroy those emails I gave you.
Why did you leak them to the press?
                         (beat)
Anyway, I'm in a tight spot, and I need to get rid of some
more.

                         WALLACE
                    (shouting out)
He's looking at me.

                                   CLINTON pulls more emails from
                                   her pocket and hands them over.

                         CLINTON
I'll pay you later.

                                   CLINTON returns to the stage.

                         CLINTON
Now, where were we?

                         WALLACE
Your emails.

                         CLINTON
That's right, the Access Hollywood tape.

                         WALLACE
Secretary Clinton --

                                             (CONTINUED)

                              CLINTON
I would be happy to clarify my position on that tape. As
I've said before, I find the words that my opponent used
absolutely horrifying, yet also in a strange way, very
beautiful.

                               TRUMP
Wrong.

                              WALLACE
Mister Trump.

                               TRUMP
It was just locker room talk. I know because I am the best
person in the world at locker room talk. I am actually so
great at locker room talk that I will soon be releasing a
new book --

                              WALLACE
Mister Trump, please --

                                        TRUMP reaches for a giant book
                                        from under his podium and holds
                                        it up, the cover reading "Locker
                                        Room Talk by Donald J. Trump."

                               TRUMP
Called Locker Room Talk. It is a picture book, and it will
have pictures in it. It is going to have pictures of…

                                        He turns to a page to reveal a
                                        picture of a cat.

                               TRUMP
Cats.
                         (beat)
Why does it have a cat in it? I knew I should not have left
Eric Trump to put this together. What is on this page?

                                        Turning the page, there's a
                                        diagram of a vagina labeled
                                        "Mrs. Eric."

                                                          (CONTINUED)

                         TRUMP
A missus Eric. And what about this page?

                                   Turning again, there's a photo
                                   of himself.

                         TRUMP
Me.

                                   Beat, and then he puts the book
                                   away.

                         TRUMP
I think we should move on, Mister Christopher Wallace.

                         WALLACE
I agree, Mister Trump. Let's move on now to our final
question of the night --

                         CLINTON
Oh, one moment. I just need a drink of water.

                                   She brings a small glass of
                                   water from under her podium and
                                   drinks from it.

                         TRUMP
I too also need water.

                                   TRUMP brings up his own,
                                   slightly bigger glass, and
                                   drinks using both hands.

                         TRUMP
I only drink the best and wettest water.

                                   CLINTON reaches for a still
                                   bigger glass and drinks.

                                   TRUMP watches for a moment then
                                   reaches for an even bigger
                                   glass. As he drinks, his hands
                                   shake.

                                                    (CONTINUED)

                              WALLACE
Mister Trump, what are you doing?

                                        CLINTON reaches for yet another
                                        bigger glass and drinks.

                                        Refusing to give in, TRUMP
                                        reaches for a bucket of water,
                                        brings it to his face, his hands
                                        shaking, and attempts to drink
                                        but ends up pouring it down
                                        himself.

                              TRUMP
I need a towel.

                              WALLACE
I don't have a towel, Mister Trump.

                              CLINTON
Don't worry, Donald, I've got one you can have. I thought
we might need one tonight, we all know how old men like you
can be at times.

                                        CLINTON reaches for a towel and
                                        throws it to TRUMP. He opens it,
                                        and without noticing the "I'm
                                        With Her" slogan on the other
                                        side, dries himself and throws
                                        the towel offstage.

                              WALLACE
Am I able to continue with the question now, or would you
like to go for a paddle, Mister Trump?

                              CLINTON
                           (laughing hard)
Ha! That's a really funny joke.

                              TRUMP
I do not get it.

                                                        (CONTINUED)

WALLACE

And so our final question of the evening, what qualities do
you think you each have that make you suitable for the role
of President of the United States?
(a pause)
And so that concludes tonight's debate, thank you to --

CLINTON

Wait! I've got one.

WALLACE

Well, do enlighten us, Secretary Clinton.

CLINTON

I am not Donald Trump.

WALLACE

Is that all you've got, Secretary Clinton?

TRUMP

Oh, no.

CLINTON
(smiling)
I could instead tell you about all of my achievements,
including those while I was First Lady, or my response on
nine eleven as a New York Senator, or those while I was
this great nation's Secretary of State. Did you know that I
played a part in ridding the world of Osama Bin Laden?
Right after it happened, I got the very eighth fist bump
with Barack Obama as we celebrated. But why do I need to
mention any of those? Is not being a balding old orange
racist who clearly volunteers as the mop for a local dog
grooming salon, not enough?

WALLACE

Well, that is for the voters to decide, Secretary Clinton.
Mister Trump, do you have anything to say? What qualities
do you have that make you suitable to be president?

TRUMP

Can I phone a friend?

(CONTINUED)

                         WALLACE
We've already told you, Mister Trump, it costs three
dollars a minute to call Moscow.

                         TRUMP
Can I call a local friend?

                         WALLACE
It's not customary in a presidential debate, but if you
promise to be quick, we'll make an exception.

                              CONWAY enters holding a large
                              toy phone.

                         CONWAY
What's the number, sir?

                              As he speaks, TRUMP holds up the
                              wrong number on his hand each
                              time.

                         TRUMP
Two-one-two-eight-three-six-three-two-four-nine.

                              CONWAY dials, and the phone
                              rings out.

                         RECORDED VOICE (OFF)
                         (in Russian accent)
Hello, you're through to the Trump Grill at Trump Tower.
Visit now and ask for our special, the triple nothing
burger with treasoning. We promise Eric hasn't touched it.

Here at the Trump Grill, we now accept roubles.
                         (beat)
Press one to make a reservation. Press two to inquire about
our menu. Press three if you are a foreign dictator and
wish to pay your deposit to secure a meeting with Donald
Trump. Press four if you have dirt on Hillary Clinton.
Press five to speak to the manager.

                         TRUMP
Press five.

                                             (CONTINUED)

>   CONWAY presses, and it continues
>   to ring until JUNIOR answers.

                          JUNIOR (OFF)
Hello, you're through to the manager of the Trump Grill at
Trump Tower... What are you wearing?

                          TRUMP
                     (on phone)
Donald Trump Junior, I am just one question away from
making myself billions --

                          JUNIOR (OFF)
I thought we were both going to be rich when you become
president?

                          TRUMP
                     (on phone)
That is right, making us billions.

                          JUNIOR (OFF)
Okay, what's the question? I'll try to help.

                          TRUMP
                     (on phone)
What qualities do I, Donald J. Trump, have that make me
suitable to be president?

                          JUNIOR (OFF)
Is it multiple choice?

                          TRUMP
                     (to WALLACE)
Is it multiple choice, Christopher Wallace?

                          WALLACE
No, Mister Trump, it is not multiple choice.

                          TRUMP
                     (on phone)
No, it is not multiple choice.

                          JUNIOR (OFF)
Well, can you ask the audience?

                                              (CONTINUED)

                         TRUMP
                       (on phone)
We are in Las Vegas, this is not my crowd. Here they prefer
casino owners who do not go bankrupt.

                      JUNIOR (OFF)
Here's what I think you should do. Ignore the question and
just say something outrageous.

                         TRUMP
                       (on phone)
I'll try it.

                         The call ends, and CONWAY exits.

                         TRUMP
He said I should just be myself.
                       (beat)
Crooked Hillary Clinton is a nasty woman, and I would only
give her a three.

                        CLINTON
This is just typical Donald Trump, isn't it? But as my
friend Michelle Obama says, when he goes low, we should go
high, and personally, I'd give Donald ten.

                        WALLACE
You would give him ten, Secretary Clinton?

                         TRUMP
I did not know you thought I looked that good.

                        CLINTON
Looks? I didn't know we were talking about looks. I thought
we were on about electoral votes.

                         A gong sounds.

                        WALLACE
Oh, and that is our indication that we have run out of time
for this debate.

                                              (CONTINUED)

                         CLINTON
Well, I'm off to the White House. I've got to measure the
curtains.

ACT I, SCENE THIRTEEN | CLINTON & OBAMA

                              A WHITE HOUSE OFFICE where
                              CLINTON and OBAMA sit talking.

                         NARRATOR
                        (entering)
With the three debates over it's three-zero to team blue
and a reputation of terror sticking to Trump like a
particularly strong glue.

For Clinton, what can go wrong? Nobody knows. Her
Presidency is a certainty with a percentage that only
grows.

The campaigns have been long, but there are still some days
for both to go. But first, for Hillary, there's time for a
meeting not for sorrow or show, but with a man who is now
her mentor and friend, and no longer a foe.

                         The NARRATOR exits.

                         CLINTON
And then, you'll never believe this, Barack, he said that
no one respects women more than him.

                         OBAMA
In fact, Hillary, as it so happens, I did actually see him
making the comment that you are referring to there... I was
watching that rally of his on my electrical television set
over in the White House Residence... It's just out of this
door, through another, outside, left and then straight on
past the bush that looks suspiciously like a Russian spy
wearing camouflage... But despite having witnessed Donald
Trump making the claim that you have just reported in your
own words... I do still find it hard to believe, which, as
you know, is an unusual thing for me... because always in
my administration I have strived to see... the best in
people.

                                             (CONTINUED)

                         CLINTON
Yes, yes, but do you know what else he said?

                         OBAMA
Yes, Hillary, I do know... but in order to avoid a social
conflict or any form of tension... how about you remind me
in words that are rendered from your own free thought?

                         CLINTON
He said that he would be the most qualified president ever.

                         OBAMA
Now that really is quite funny... it's like a joke. A funny
joke.

                                   As they laugh, the NARRATOR
                                   enters, takes a photo of them,
                                   then exits.

                         CLINTON
What was that? They had a camera. Why is there someone with
a camera?

                         OBAMA
That was a photographer that I arranged... I thought it
would be a good idea if we could put out a photo of you
laughing... and looking human.

                         CLINTON
Why? Don't I normally look human? I'm a human. I look
human. People think I'm human.
                    (beat)
Hey, Barack, would you mind putting out a formal statement
confirming that I'm human?

                         OBAMA
Putting out a statement of words from our English
language... that achieve such a purpose is certainly
something that I would be willing... to look at doing for
you.

                         CLINTON
Thanks, Barack. Where would I be without you?

                                                      (CONTINUED)

CONTINUED:

                         OBAMA
You would have been president eight years ago.

                              COOPER enters on a moving desk.

                         COOPER
Hello, you're watching C-N-N, and I'm Anderson Cooper here
with breaking news.

                         OBAMA
                        (waving)
Well good post afternoon to you, Anderson.

                         COOPER
                      (waving back)
President Obama, sir.
                      (to audience)
This just in. F-B-I director, James Comey, has today
written to Congress to inform them that he is re-opening
the investigation into the use of private emails by Hillary
Clinton.

                         Beat.

                         CLINTON
I'm sorry. I'm not sure I heard that.

                         COOPER
In a letter that was addressed to the Chair of the House
Intelligence Committee, Mister Comey confirmed the F-B-I
has uncovered new emails that were not included as part of
the first investigation, which later concluded after
finding no wrongdoing from the former Secretary of State.
While it is not known the extent of the new evidence these
new emails contain, it will surely have a negative impact
on the Clinton campaign just a few days out from the
election.
                        (beat)
Duck.

                              He ducks and is narrowly missed
                              an object thrown by CLINTON.

                                            (CONTINUED)

CONTINUED:

                         COOPER
That's all from me for now.

                         COOPER and his desk exit.

                         OBAMA
Hillary, are you okay? That news there... it didn't sound
as though it would please a person such as yourself... at
the present time.

                         A pause.

                         CLINTON
I... I just need a moment. I need a moment, Barack.

                         CLINTON exits, screams, and then
                         returns to the stage.

                         OBAMA
Hillary?

                         CLINTON
This is --

                         OBAMA
Hillary?

                         CLINTON
Going to be okay.

                         OBAMA
Are you sure that there is truth in the words you are
using?

                         CLINTON
This is going to be okay. I can still win. America isn't
stupid. I can win this. I can do this.

                         OBAMA
What if you don't?

                                                  (CONTINUED)

                          CLINTON
If I don't?
                    (beat)
Then I will personally see to it that I get revenge.

ACT I, SCENE FOURTEEN | ELECTION DAY

                          First, a NEW YORK POLLING
                          STATION where TRUMP and
                          CARDBOARD MELANIA TRUMP are
                          voting. Nearby, CONWAY (in
                          disguise), and an ELECTION
                          OFFICIAL.

                          NARRATOR
                    (entering)
The eighth day of November, one to go down in history, for
today is the day America elects its first woman as
president or the day it elects it by a landslide. No matter
the news of emails, the voters don't care, or so the polls
say. The result of the vote's expected to go only one way.
So what will go wrong? That is the question as we reach the
start of the day that is America's General Election.

                    COOPER enters.

                          COOPER
Thank you, Narrator. I can take it from here.

                    The NARRATOR exits.

                          COOPER
Good morning to all of you, it's November eighth, I'm
Anderson Cooper reporting here for C-N-N, and I can tell
you all, I'm looking forward to getting my sticker later
today.

                    HOLT enters.

                          HOLT
Hello America. Lester Holt here for N-B-C on what is set to
be a historic day for the country.
                    (MORE)

                                              (CONTINUED)

CONTINUED:

                        HOLT (CONT'D)
Are we getting our first president who is a woman, or are
we getting our first who is a high contrast sitcom
character?

                    RADDATZ enters.

                        RADDATZ
Martha Raddatz here for A-B-C, good morning America. Well,
it's election day again, don't forget to get out and vote.

                        STEVE DOOCY, AINSLEY EARHARDT,
                        and BRIAN KILMEADE all enter.

                        DOOCY
Good morning, Steve Doocy here.

                        EARHARDT
I heard that it's a good morning too, Steve. I'm Ainsley
Earhardt.

                        KILMEADE
I'm Brian Kilmeade, and last night, I had to go to the
emergency room because when I tried to pick my nose, my
finger got stuck.

                        EARHARDT
That's a funny story, Brian. Welcome to Fox and Friends,
everyone.

                        KILMEADE
I don't have any friends, Ainsley.

                        DOOCY
What beautiful weather we have this election day, certainly
here in New York City where we're joining Republican
candidate, Donald J. Trump as he casts his own vote. I
wonder who he voted for?

                        EARHARDT
You know, Steve? I'm wondering that too. Ahaha.

                                            (CONTINUED)
PERFORMANCE LICENSE EDITION   LICENSE # _ _ _ _ _ _ _ _

                    KILMEADE
I voted earlier, but I don't want anyone to know that I
voted for Donald Trump, so I kept my ballot paper in my
pocket.

                    COOPER
I'm in New York City this morning, just a few blocks away
from where stands the Fifth Avenue tower that Donald Trump
calls home. Will he still be calling it home after today?
The polls certainly say so.

                    HOLT
The Republican nominee and his wife are here about to cast
their own votes in this historic election.

                    RADDATZ
I'm sure we need no panel of experts to discuss how they
will be doing so.

                              TRUMP looks across to see who
                              CARDBOARD MELANIA is voting for.

                    TRUMP
Oh good. You're voting the same as me.

                              TRUMP takes his ballot and
                              places it in the box.

                    DOOCY
You know guys, I wonder if Mister Trump would be willing to
talk to us quickly?

                    EARHARDT
I'm wondering that too, Steve. What do you think, Brian?

                    KILMEADE
I don't think, Ainsley.

                    All three wave at TRUMP.

                    DOOCY
Hey, Mister Trump.

                                             (CONTINUED)

97.

                         EARHARDT
I also say hello to Mister Trump, Steve.

                         KILMEADE
Ahoy-hoy.

                              TRUMP walks to them while
                              behind, CARDBOARD MELANIA "runs
                              off."
                         TRUMP
Hello Steve Doocy, Ainsley Earhardt and, sorry, I forgot
your name.

                         KILMEADE
I'm Donald Trump. It's good to see you today, Brian
Kilmeade.

                         TRUMP
It is great to be here, Donald Trump.

                         RADDATZ
First on A-B-C --

                         HOLT
Breaking news just in --

                         COOPER
Dang it.

                         HOLT
Too slow, Anderson.

                         COOPER
Third on C-N-N, Hillary Clinton has arrived to cast her own
vote.

                         CLINTON enters.

                         CLINTON
Hello everyone. It's Hillary Rodham Clinton here.

                              COOPER, HOLT, and RADDATZ rush
                              to her.

                                        (CONTINUED)
PERFORMANCE LICENSE EDITION   LICENSE # _ _ _ _ _ _ _ _

CONTINUED:

                         HOLT
Secretary Clinton.

                         CLINTON
Hello, Lester, Martha, good to see you both again. Oh, and
we have Anderson here too.

                         HOLT
Last again, Cooper.

                         COOPER
We'll see who's last when the ratings come in, Holt.

                         TRUMP
Ratings? Did someone mention ratings?

                         DOOCY
So, Mister Trump, can you tell us who you voted for today?

                         TRUMP
Steve Doocy, let me tell you who I did not vote for. I did
not vote for that woman over there.
               (pointing at CLINTON)
That woman, not a lot of people know this, is my opponent,
Hillary Clinton, okay. Unlike me, she is not so great. She
is bad and evil and nasty and crooked and a woman. I would
never vote for her. In fact, I would never vote for her so
much that so show it, I put a big cross, like a huge no, in
the box next to her name on my ballot paper, and I
encourage all of my supporters to do the same.
               (turning back)
And my wife, who is just here -- Wait, where did she go?

                         CLINTON
Hey, Donald, you know that by putting a cross next to my
name, you actually voted for me?

                         TRUMP
What?

                         DOOCY
I think she might be right, Mister Trump.

                                              (CONTINUED)

                          EARHARDT
I think so too, Steve, which is unusual because Hillary is
a woman and we all know what we think about that here on
Fox and Friends...

                          KILMEADE
I drew a picture of a bumblebee in the box to cast my vote.

                          EARHARDT
No, Brian. That is not what we all think.

                              TRUMP approaches the ELECTION
                              OFFICIAL.

                          TRUMP
Hello, election people. I hereby demand that I get to vote
again. I voted for the wrong person.

                          ELECTION OFFICIAL
I'm sorry, Mister Trump, but I can't allow that. There's no
way for us to know which ballot you put in the box.

                          TRUMP
It is the one marked in crayon.

                          ELECTION OFFICIAL
I can't help you, sir.

                          TRUMP
This is rigged. This whole election is rigged.

                          CONWAY
                     (removing her disguise)
Yes, it is, Mister Trump. But we're not supposed to let
everyone know.

                              As she puts her disguise back
                              on, the NARRATOR enters.

                          NARRATOR
Six hours until the polls close.

                                                    (CONTINUED)
PERFORMANCE LICENSE EDITION   LICENSE # _ _ _ _ _ _ _ _

CONTINUED:

                              The NARRATOR exits with CLINTON,
                              CONWAY, and TRUMP, and the
                              action moves to a WISCONSIN
                              POLLING STATION.

                         COOPER
It's been an eventful election day so far as millions have
turned out across the country to have their say.

                          HOLT
But as we all know, it's the swing states that really
matter on days like this. States like Florida.

                         COOPER
Once every four years isn't bad.

                         RADDATZ
To bring you the latest coverage on the way the country is
swinging, I'm at a polling station in the swing state of
Wisconsin.

                              A WISCONSIN VOTER enters and
                              HOLT approaches.

                          HOLT
Lester Holt from N-B-C. Can I ask you how you voted today?

                     WISCONSIN VOTER
Yes, you can ask me.

                          HOLT
Thank you. How did you vote today?

                     WISCONSIN VOTER
I voted for Hillary Clinton.

                          HOLT
And can you talk about why you voted that way?

                     WISCONSIN VOTER
She didn't visit us that much, and if she's considerate
enough not to make us listen to her, she gets my vote.

                              HOLT bows towards COOPER.

                                             (CONTINUED)
PERFORMANCE LICENSE EDITION   LICENSE # _ _ _ _ _ _ _

                        HOLT
Exclusive insight, only on N-B-C.

                        EARHARDT
Guys, what are we doing here in Wisconsin?

                        KILMEADE
I've been to Wisconsin once before. It's just like Michigan
except it's not Michigan, it's Wisconsin.

                        DOOCY
Well, Ainsley, we were here to talk to Paul Ryan, but did
you know he wasn't able to cast his vote today?

                        EARHARDT
I did know that, Steve. But do you know why he wasn't able
to vote?

                        DOOCY
Yes, I do know, Ainsley. It's because a voter decided to
ask him a question about healthcare on his way to vote and
so he was forced to run away.

                        EARHARDT
It's so inconsiderate of the voter. How dare they ask the
Speaker of the House for his views on a major topic.

                        DOOCY
Especially on election day.

                        EARHARDT
Especially on election day, Steve.

                        KILMEADE
I don't think there's anything wrong with healthcare in
this country. Whenever I go to the doctor, they always give
me a sticker for not crying.

                                    COOPER pulls out and begins
                                    looking on his phone.

                        COOPER
                     (looking up)
I bet you haven't got this one, Holt.
                        (MORE)
                                                    (CONTINUED)

CONTINUED:

COOPER (CONT'D)
(beat)
Breaking news on C-N-N...

HOLT
A dog in San Diego has learned how to jet ski. An exclusive
first on N-B-C.

COOPER
Oh, come on!

     HOLT begins to point into the
     wings.

HOLT
Look, Anderson. There's a breaking story in the distance.

     COOPER begins to look.

COOPER
Where?

     COOPER exits into the wings.

DOOCY
So what do you guys think about voters requiring a form of
photo I-D to be allowed to vote?

EARHARDT
I think that it's a good idea, Steve. We don't want all
those nasty illegals making no difference by all voting in
a state Hillary Clinton is already guaranteed to win.

DOOCY
That's right, Ainsley.

KILMEADE
I heard they can't take voter's photos in Pennsylvania
because everyone there is a vampire.

EARHARDT
That's Transylvania, Brian, not Pennsylvania.

(CONTINUED)

>   A badly disguised PUTIN enters
>   and approaches the ELECTION
>   OFFICIAL.

                         PUTIN
Hello. I be here to vote.

                         ELECTION OFFICIAL
Can I take your name?

                         PUTIN
Mister A person.

                         ELECTION OFFICIAL
Here's your ballot.

>   PUTIN takes the ballot, marks
>   it, places it in the box then
>   moves to center stage.

                         PUTIN
I'm ready.

>   DMITRY and PETROV run on stage
>   with a screen to block him from
>   view.
>
>   There is a pause while he
>   changes.

                         PUTIN
I'm done.

>   DMITRY and PETROV exit to reveal
>   PUTIN now dressed as a farmer.
>   He approaches the ELECTION
>   OFFICIAL.

                         PUTIN
Well, howdy there partners. I'm be here to cast my olde
vote.

                         ELECTION OFFICIAL
Can I take your name?

                                              (CONTINUED)

PUTIN

Mister A farmer.

ELECTION OFFICIAL

Here's your ballot.

> PUTIN takes the ballot, marks
> it, and places it in the box.
>
> The NARRATOR enters.

NARRATOR

Polls closed.

> The NARRATOR exits.

RADDATZ

And that is it, the voting is over. All we can do now is
wait for the results as they come in.

HOLT

And those results will be coming in on N-B-C all night
long.

ACT I, SCENE FIFTEEN | THE RESULTS

> And those results will be coming
> in on N-B-C all night long.

NARRATOR
(entering)
While the polls may have closed, it's still early in the
night, and both sides remain more than ready and up to
continue their fight. For as all across the country, the
counting begins, both team red and team blue wait up to see
who wins.

CLINTON

Oh, I'm so nervous. What if I only win by two hundred
electoral votes?

BILL

Then we'll be drug testing the entire population of Texas.

                                              (CONTINUED)

CONTINUED:

                          NARRATOR
And so as we journey forth to find out who has won the
states in the south and those in the north, who better to
set our course than Anderson Cooper, C-N-N's number one
anchor, and from Fox News, their number one --
                          (beat)
Sean Hannity.

                               COOPER and SEAN HANNITY enter
                               and flank the NARRATOR.

                          COOPER
Good evening. I'm Anderson Cooper, and no, I do not know
how Lester Holt ended up on a non-stop to South America.

                          HANNITY
You're watching Hannity with me, Sean Hannity. Tonight, is
the grass really green, or is it just a liberal conspiracy?
That coming up later, but first, it's going to be a long
night, no worry for me, of course, I've got my trusty
Keurig coffee in hand, those guys will never let me down.
It's the two thousand and sixteen election.

                          NARRATOR
Delaware.

                          COOPER
And that's it, we're off with the first result of the
night, and it's a win for Hillary Clifton in Delaware as
she takes the lead in the electoral college.

                          HANNITY
The election will have to wait though as we kick off with
our top story of the night. And we're going to San Diego
where a dog has, get this, learned to jet ski. Is it just a
smart Republican dog? Or is Hillary Clinton training up an
army of animals to go against the American people?

                          NARRATOR
Indiana.

                          COOPER
And with the second result in, it's ten votes from Indiana
to Trump, putting him in the lead.

                                              (CONTINUED)

PERFORMANCE LICENSE EDITION   LICENSE # _ _ _ _ _ _ _ _

                         HANNITY
I guess we'll just have to wait and see because right now
we've just heard that Donald J. Trump has taken the lead in
the electoral college with a win in his running mate, Mike
Pence's home state.

                         NARRATOR
New York.

                         COOPER
With a win in both her and her opponent's home state,
Hillary Clinton has taken the lead.

                         HANNITY
We now return to San Diego.

                         NARRATOR
Texas.

                         COOPER
And with Texas in it's now a narrow lead for Donald Trump.

                         HANNITY
Breaking news, Hillary Clinton is a loser.

                         NARRATOR
California.

                         COOPER
As expected, a big boost for Hillary Clinton here.

                         HANNITY
Well, screw the dog in San Diego. Let's admire this video
of Ted Cruz cooking bacon on a gun instead.

                         NARRATOR
Wisconsin.

                         COOPER
They've previously elected Paul Ryan, and clearly, they
never learn. It's a boost for Trump here, but Clinton still
leads.

                                              (CONTINUED)

                         HANNITY
That really is some beautiful bacon.

                         NARRATOR
Alabama and Oklahoma.

                         HANNITY
Two great placed both voting red, that's sixteen electoral
votes for Donald J. Trump.

                         COOPER
A number which some of them, thanks to their unique
genetics, are able to count on their sixteen fingers across
both of their three hands.

                         NARRATOR
D-C, Nevada, Washington, Vermont, New Jersey.

                         COOPER
And Secretary Clinton is still in the lead.

                         HANNITY
I want to now spend some time discussing one of the major
issues that old white men face in the office. Do you draft
the non-disclosure agreement before or after?

                         NARRATOR
Alaska, Kentucky, North Dakota, Ohio, West Virginia,
Tennessee, Michigan, Utah, Montana, and Louisiana.

                         HANNITY
Staying on that subject, Donald Trump has retaken the lead
in the electoral college.

                         NARRATOR
Maryland, Colorado, Connecticut, New Mexico, Oregon, Rhode
Island, Nebraska, Virginia.

                         COOPER
We're calling all of these for Clinton on C-N-N.

                         HANNITY
We're calling all of these traitors on Fox News.

                                                    (CONTINUED)

CONTINUED:

                         NARRATOR
Maine.

                         COOPER
One vote to Trump and three to Clinton here.

                         NARRATOR
Arizona, South Carolina, North Carolina.

                         COOPER
Called for Donald Trump.

                         HANNITY
Called for Donald Trump.

                         NARRATOR
Georgia, Idaho, Kansas, Iowa, South Dakota.

                         HANNITY
Get this, Trump is leading the electoral college.

                         NARRATOR
Illinois, Minnesota, New Hampshire.

                         COOPER
We're calling these three for Hillary Clinton, but she
still trails behind. If she can just win in Missouri,
Arkansas, Mississippi, and Wyoming, she'll take the lead
again.

                         NARRATOR
Missouri.

                         HANNITY
Called for Donald Trump.

                         NARRATOR
Arkansas.

                         HANNITY
Donald Trump.

                         NARRATOR
Mississippi.

                                              (CONTINUED)

                        HANNITY
It's Donald Trump.

                        NARRATOR
Wyoming.

                        HANNITY
Again, we're calling it for Donald Trump.

                        COOPER
I need to call for a change of pants.

                        NARRATOR
Pennsylvania.

                        COOPER
Called for Donald Trump.

                    All on stage stop and stare at
                    COOPER.

                        HANNITY
What?

                        NARRATOR
What?

                        CLINTON
What?

                        OBAMA
Now, what is going on there? That result makes no sense...
It's like an onion in a fruit salad.

                        TRUMP
Losers. Pennsylvania is just full of losers.

                        JUNIOR
Dad, you won the state.

                        TRUMP
Wait, what?

                                              (CONTINUED)

CONTINUED:

                          NARRATOR
Florida.

                          COOPER
It's the final result of the night, and it's just come in.
Florida is this year swinging red.

                          OBAMA
                     (standing)
Oh...

                          COOPER
C-N-N is calling it. With Clinton at two hundred and twenty-
seven votes...

                          OBAMA
My...

                          COOPER
Donald J. Trump is going to be the forty-fifth President of
the United States.

                          OBAMA
GOD!

                    Lights out.

                  END OF ACT I

                                                    (CONTINUED)

ACT II : "THE FIRST YEAR"

ACT II, SCENE ONE | ACT II OPENING

>   With the audience seated once
>   again, the lights across the
>   auditorium go down, and the
>   anticipation is allowed to build
>   on the empty stage before a
>   single spotlight shines, and the
>   music begins.

                         NARRATOR
                         (entering)
/YOU MIGHT BE THINKING YOU'RE IN THR WRONG SHOW, BUT NO
NEED TO WORRY, FOR THIS IS JUST A PARODY SONG, WHICH JUST
LIKE THIS PARODY PRESIDENT SHOULDN'T LAST LONG.

A TREASONOUS RACIST, MISOGYNIST, ALL TOGETHER HATED MAN IN
THE WHITE HOUSE, WHAT - THE - HELL'S - HE - TWEETED - NOW?/

>   A light goes up on CLINTON, who
>   stands drinking from a bottle of
>   wine.

                         CLINTON
/CAN WE ALL SCREAM NOW?/

                         NARRATOR
                         (gesturing at the bottle)
Please?

>   The NARRATOR takes the bottle,
>   drinks from it, and then hands
>   it back before she exits.

                         NARRATOR
/YOU CAN'T BELIEVE IT YET, YOU HAVEN'T HAD THE CHANCE, HIS
WHOLE VOTER BASE IS CLEARLY IN A TRANCE, AND SOMEHOW HE
CAN'T EVEN FIND TO WEAR, CORRECTLY - FITTING - PANTS./

>   The stage fills with light as
>   the ENSEMBLE stand in a line.

                                             (CONTINUED)

CONTINUED:

                              In front of them, TRUMP, his
                              pants clearly too tight.

                         ENSEMBLE
/DONALD TRUMP IS AN ORANGE MAN (WITH VERY TINY HANDS), AND
HE HAS RACIST FANS --/

                          TRUMP
WAIT!

                              The music stops, and the
                              ENSEMBLE clear the stage.

                          TRUMP
I do not like this song. This song is from a show I do not
like, which I hear is highly overrated and also not so
great. The cast was also very mean to Mike Pence, and Mike
Pence deserves better. He has had a very tough life
because, for the last fifty-seven years, he has had to live
as Mike Pence.

                        NARRATOR
Mister President-Elect --

                          TRUMP
No one, except the audience of this show perhaps, has ever
had a tougher time in a theater than Mike Pence. Especially
no politician.

                        NARRATOR
What about President Abraham Lincoln?

                              Beat.

                        CLINTON
                     (leaning on stage)
I just want to say, I like that show. I'm down with that
relatable stuff. I love rap, it's what Bill and I order as
a sandwich when we feel adventurous.

                          TRUMP
Go away, Crooked Hillary Clinton.

                              CLINTON exits.

                                              (CONTINUED)

CONTINUED:

                          TRUMP
Can we sing something different?

                          NARRATOR
Sure, I've got another.

                              The NARRATOR stamps their foot.

                              The music begins, and the
                              ENSEMBLE enters wearing TRUMP
                              masks.

                          ENSEMBLE
/TRUMPY LUMPY TRUMPETY DOO, HE...
                      (pointing at TRUMP)
DOESN'T GIVE A DAMN ABOUT YOU.
                      (pointing at the audience)
TRUMPY LUMPY TRUMPETY DEE.../

                              Stepping forward and removing
                              their mask, one of the ENSEMBLE
                              reveal themselves as PUTIN.

                          PUTIN
                  (bringing a tape from his
                  pocket)
/I HAVE TAPE WHERE HE BE COVERED IN PEE./

                              The music stops, and the
                              ENSEMBLE clear to leave the
                              NARRATOR, PUTIN, and TRUMP.

                          TRUMP
What tape?

                          PUTIN
Well, Donald, that tape.

                          TRUMP
But you cannot have that tape. It does not exist.

                          PUTIN
                  (holding the tape up)
It exist. I have tape here. It show you covered in pee-pee.

                                              (CONTINUED)

                          TRUMP
I do not remember that happening.

                          PUTIN
Really, do you not? What about in Moscow?

                          TRUMP
I do not remember being in Moscow.

                          PUTIN
In Ritz Carlton hotel?

                          TRUMP
I do not remember staying at the Ritz Carlton hotel.

                          PUTIN
In presidential suite?

                          TRUMP
I do not remember staying in the presidential suite.

                          PUTIN
Their names be Dominika and Kristina.

                          Beat.

                          TRUMP
I remember.
                    (moving closer)
Do you have the bit where?

                          PUTIN
Yes.

                          TRUMP
What about the bit where they --

                          PUTIN
Yes.

                          TRUMP
How about the bit where --

                                              (CONTINUED)
PERFORMANCE LICENSE EDITION   LICENSE # _ _ _ _ _ _ _ _

                         PUTIN
I have all of it, Donald.

                         TRUMP
Even the bit where...

                              TRUMP whispers into PUTIN'S ear,
                              and PUTIN's expression turns to
                              one of disgust.

                         PUTIN
No. I not know you did that.
                    (beat)
You are it after?

                              PUTIN notices the NARRATOR stood
                              watching them.

                         PUTIN
Hello, Narrator. May I ask you, would you care to see
people you know ever again?

                         NARRATOR
Yes, I would.

                         PUTIN
Then listen to me. You need to help out old Uncle Putin, do
you understand?

                         NARRATOR
Yes.

                         PUTIN
Good, then I need you, as I believe you put it in west...
go away and tell no one about what you just heard. Do you
still understand me?

                         NARRATOR
I think so.

                         PUTIN
Good. Then go away.

                              The NARRATOR exits.

                                             (CONTINUED)

CONTINUED:

                         PUTIN
Now then, Donald.

                         TRUMP
Yes, Comrade Vladimir Putin, sir.

                         PUTIN
We need to talk.

                         TRUMP
Are you breaking up with America?

                         PUTIN
No. Why would I break up with America? It take big effort
to rig election?
                    (beat)
But there be things that I need to make sure you understand
now that you be President of United States.

                         TRUMP
Yes, Comrade, sir.

                         PUTIN
Number one. You belong to Putin.

                    Beat.

                         TRUMP
What is number two?

                         PUTIN
There be no number two. Putin not want to confuse you with
big numbers.

                         TRUMP
Thank you, Comrade Vladimir Putin, sir.

                         PUTIN
I own you now, Donald. You do Putin say when Putin tell
you. Do you understand me?

                         TRUMP
Yes, sir.

                                              (CONTINUED)

CONTINUED:

                         PUTIN
And should you fail to obey, this tape of golden moment of
become public.

                         TRUMP
I will do whatever you say.

                         PUTIN
Very good. I see message has gotten across. Kneel.

                         TRUMP
What?

                         PUTIN
I said kneel.

                    TRUMP kneels before him.

                         PUTIN
Now crawl offstage.

                    TRUMP does as he's told.

                         PUTIN
                       (to audience)
I know where all of you live also.

                    PUTIN exits.

ACT II, SCENE TWO | TRUMP MEETS WITH OBAMA

                         At first, a dark and empty
                         stage.

                         NARRATOR
                       (entering)
Well, I think we can all agree that got weird.
                       (beat)
And so it is that with the election over, the world sits in
shock, for America has elected to get a new president who
all expect to run amok.
                         (MORE)

                                              (CONTINUED)

CONTINUED:

                    NARRATOR (CONT'D)
But before we can reach the day of his inauguration, a day
which many feel can never come too late, the new President-
Elect is off to meet with the man who previously, he had
feelings toward of nothing but hate.

                              As the NARRATOR exits, lights go
                              up on the OVAL OFFICE, where the
                              ENSEMBLE (as PRESS) sit in front
                              of TRUMP, who himself is sat
                              waiting next to an empty chair.

                    TRUMP
Do any of you know where he is? I thought he would be here
by now. He said he would be here ten minutes ago. I know
some people would call this late. I would never say that,
but some people would. I guess we do have to let him off,
right? He does have a long commute. Did you know that the
guy flies in from Kenya every morning?

                              A spotlight finds OBAMA at the
                              other side of the stage drinking
                              shots. After a moment, he slaps
                              himself on the face and then
                              walks over to TRUMP.

                    TRUMP
                    (standing)
Oh, here is he. He has made it. Mister President, it is
good to see you.

                    OBAMA
Oh... my... god...

                         They both sit.

                    PRESS #1
Mister President, Mister President-Elect, how are you both
feeling about last night's result?

                    TRUMP
                    (to OBAMA)
Would you like to start?

                                                  (CONTINUED)

PERFORMANCE LICENSE EDITION   LICENSE # _ _ _ _ _ _ _ _

                         OBAMA
Oh... my... god...

                         TRUMP
I guess I am starting then. Well, press journalist person,
I do not know your name --

                         PRESS #1
It's Rachel, I'm from C-N-N --

                         TRUMP
Fake news. You are fake news. I do not care about your
name, but I do care that I am very pleased about the result
last night. It was great, it could not have gone any more
great, it was just fantastic.

                    OBAMA lets out an audible groan.

                         TRUMP
                      (to OBAMA)
Would you like to say anything?

                         OBAMA
Oh... my... god...

                         TRUMP
I think we are ready for the next question.

                         PRESS #2
Mister President-Elect, you've made quite a few strongly-
worded statements over the years about the President, often
criticizing his judgments and actions. So will you be
calling on him for advice as you enter office yourself?

                         TRUMP
That is fake news. I have never said anything bad about
this man.

                         OBAMA
Oh... my... god...

PERFORMANCE LICENSE EDITION   LICENSE # _ _ _ _ _ _ _ _

                         PRESS #2
Mister Trump, that simply isn't true. In the past you have
spent years leading a moment questioning where the
President was born, you have accused him of being the
founder of ISIS, and you have said multiple times that you
feel he is the worse leader that America has ever had.

                         TRUMP
Correct. Fake news. Next question.

                         PRESS #3
President Obama, have you had the chance to speak to
Secretary Clinton this morning? Do you know if she's doing
okay?

                              A scream comes from somewhere
                              backstage.

                         OBAMA
Oh... my... god...

                         CLINTON (OFF)
Nearly three million votes. Three million.

                              OBAMA points towards the wings
                              and stands.

                         PRESS #4
Mister President, do you need to attend to that?

                              OBAMA begins to nod then slowly
                              begins shaking his head.

                         OBAMA
Oh... my... god...

                         PRESS #4
We understand, sir.

                              OBAMA exits.

                         TRUMP
Wait, where is he going? He is being very rude toward me.

ACT II, SCENE THREE | TRUMP PICKS HIS CABINET

> TRUMP'S OFFICE on another day where CONWAY and TRUMP are mid-conversation.

CONWAY
I agree that celebrating is important, Mister Trump. But you also need to start choosing cabinet positions, sir.

TRUMP
How many do I get to choose, Kellyanne Conway?

CONWAY
You have to choose twenty-two, sir.

TRUMP
I want them all to be made out of solid gold and mounted on the wall of the Oval Office.

CONWAY
Sir?

TRUMP
One of them also needs to be really bigly so that I can fit all of my awards in it. Did you know last year I won the Trump Organization employee of the month thirteen times?

CONWAY
Mister Trump, sir, I'm talking about your government cabinet, not... cabinets.

TRUMP
I do not understand.

CONWAY
Well, the cabinet is made up of the heads of federal executive departments and a few other top advisors.

TRUMP
Like Eric Trump?

CONWAY
No, sir, that's feral.

(CONTINUED)

                         TRUMP
Okay, I want to pick Ivanka Trump, Donald Trump Junior,
Steve Bannon, and Vladimir Putin.

                         CONWAY
I'm not sure that would be appropriate. We don't want to
make it look as though you're only appointing people you
like.

                         TRUMP
What about Jeff Sessions? No one could ever believe that
someone likes Jeff Sessions?

                         CONWAY
Jeff Sessions is good. How about Ben Carlson?

                         TRUMP
It would stop him calling me asking for a job. And we
should try to look diverse.

                         CONWAY
What about Betsy DeVos too? It might be good to get a woman
in there.

                         TRUMP
I like your thinking, Kellyanne Conway.

                         CHRISTIE enters unnoticed.

                         TRUMP
I have to attend an important meeting with Kanye West right
now, can I leave the rest of the decisions to you?

                         TRUMP turns to notice CHRISTIE.

                         CHRISTIE
Hey, Mister Trump.

                         TRUMP
Chris Christie.

                         CHRISTIE
Yes, Mister Trump.

                                              (CONTINUED)

                        TRUMP

I am not choosing you. I know I said we should try to look
diverse, but we do not need to look that diverse.

                       CHRISTIE

Wow, jeez, sir. That really hurts.

ACT II, SCENE FOUR | THE PRESS CONFERENCE

                             A room in TRUMP TOWER where
                             TRUMP is stood behind a podium
                             with CONWAY next to him. In
                             front of them, the ENSEMBLE (as
                             PRESS) sit waiting.

                             At the side of the podium is a
                             table topped with papers and a
                             box.

                        TRUMP

Okay, everyone, I have called this press conference today
to tell you all about the great things I have been doing
since the election and all of the great things that I will
be doing after I am inaugurated next week.
                     (beat)
I will take questions now.

                      PRESS #1

Mister President-Elect, it's been two months since the
election, and this is the first press conference that
you've held. Can you tell us what you've been doing since
November?

                       TRUMP

No, next question.

                      PRESS #5

Mister Trump, could you tell us more about the plans for
your inauguration day? What can we expect to see?

                       TRUMP

Thank you for that question Fox News. I would be happy to
talk about all of the great things that will be happening.
                    (MORE)
                                      (CONTINUED)

TRUMPED: AN ALTERNATIVE MUSICAL   124.
PART ONE (ACT I & ACT II)
CONTINUED:

> TRUMP (CONT'D)
> You can expect to see so many great things that your mind will be blown. In the evening more great things will be happening, and it will be so great and so fantastic. We are even going to have some fireworks, which will be great, and do not worry, I have checked the immigration papers of all of the fire before they started working, okay.
>
> Also, after everyone has left, Paul Ryan, Mitch McConnell, and Donald J. Trump are going to dismantle all rights for women using executive orders.

> PRESS #2
> Mister Trump, can I ask you about the pee-pee tape?

> TRUMP
> How do you know about that?

> PRESS #2
> It was mentioned in a leaked dossier that also alleges Russia helped you to win the election.

> TRUMP
> Neither of those things is true, okay. There is no pee-pee tape, and Russia did not help me win the election. It is fake news.

> PRESS #2
> Are you sure, Mister Trump? Because we all got emailed a link to a password protected movie titled "Trump's Golden Moments."

> PRESS #3
> It also came with the note, "from Russia with love."

> PRESS #4
> Mister Trump, is this pee-pee tape going to be your Watergate?

> PRESS #2
> It's going to be his broken-Watergate.

> The ENSEMBLE laugh as CONWAY whispers to TRUMP.

(CONTINUED)

TRUMP

Okay, I want all of you to listen because we need to get
some things clear. You are all fake news losers, apart from
you, Breitbart, Fox News and Russia Today, you are all
great and you are doing a fantastic job. But from the rest
of you, I am not going to put up with your fake mainstream
media news. Let me show you something...
                    (choosing someone)
You. Where are you from?

PRESS #6

San Fransisco.

TRUMP

Then you must be a liberal from M-S-N-B-C?

PRESS #6

That's right.

TRUMP

Come up here.

                         PRESS #6 stands and moves over
                         to TRUMP.

TRUMP

Let us get something clear, okay. You are going to report
as I want you to, and the first thing you are going to
report on is how much work I have been doing. Do you see
all of these papers? You are going to tell everyone that
this is all work and that it is great.

PRESS #6
                    (checking the papers)
Mister President-Elect, these are all just blank pieces of
paper. And this box, this is probably empty...
                    (checking inside the box)
There's a horse's head in this box.

TRUMP

Casino?... I mean, capiche?

PRESS #3

Mister Trump, are you threatening us right now?

                                              (CONTINUED)

TRUMP

I could kidnap all of your families if that would help?

PRESS #1

You do know this press conference is being broadcast live, don't you?

TRUMP

Is it?

PRESS #1

Yes, Mister Trump, it is.

TRUMP
(to CONWAY)
Kellyanne Conway, we are going to need more horse's heads.

CONWAY

We don't have anymore, Mister Trump, sir. Don't you remember? You used the rest of your horses in Trump Steaks. Does your daughter have any?

TRUMP

She prefers goats, that is why she married Jared Kushner.

ACT II, SCENE FIVE | AT THE CLINTON'S

>   The CLINTON RESIDENCE, where
>   CLINTON is mid-conversation on
>   the phone.

NARRATOR
(entering)
And so it is that on the night before the inauguration, many are feeling sick, scared, and uncomfortable right across the nation. But for some time is scarce to worry, for protests in a flurry are already planned to take place tomorrow right across the land. Meanwhile, in New York's Chappaqua, a small and homely hamlet, Hillary Clinton is wondering why to get out of the inauguration nobody has a plan yet.

>   The NARRATOR exits.

(CONTINUED)

                         CLINTON
                       (on phone)
No, I got you, Jimmy. I know it's supposed to be a
tradition for all of us to go, but you know, I've spoken to
W, and he says the seniors are in hospital and being forced
to miss it. Well, we're all old, I'm sure we can catch a
cold or break a leg for the weekend... Oh, you've already
packed the Xanax? I must remember to get some of that.
                    (shouting out)
Hey, Bill, do we have any Xanax?
                      (on phone)
Hey, Jimmy, would it be okay if I was to borrow some of
yours? I'm all out. I'm sure I can bring you something in
return. How about earplugs? Oh, W's sorted those. Alcohol?
No, Barack's on that is he?

                         BILL (OFF)
Hillary.

                         CLINTON
                       (on phone)
I'll work something out. I've got to go now though, Bill's
calling me. We'll catch up properly tomorrow.

                              CLINTON ends her call as BILL
                              enters, looking excited.

                         BILL
Oh, this is going to be the best inauguration day ever.

                         CLINTON
                       (standing)
If you say that again, we're getting a divorce.

                         BILL
But Hillary, it will be. I've found it.

                         CLINTON
Found what? What have you found? Is it a hundred thousand
votes in Michigan?

                              BILL pulls a key from his
                              pocket.

                                              (CONTINUED)

CONTINUED:

                           BILL
This is better. It's my spare key to the White House.

                           Beat.

                           CLINTON
Hey, Bill, do you still have any of those whoopee cushions
left over from the time the D-N-C leadership came over for
dinner?

                                   BILL pulls a whoopee cushion
                                   from his pocket.

                           BILL
That I do, Hillary. That I do. And I've got a whole pile of
photos of us with the Obamas and some strong glue too.

                           CLINTON
I don't say this to you often enough, but William Jefferson
Clinton, I really like you sometimes.

ACT II, SCENE SIX | THE INAUGURATION

                                   THE CAPITOL, Washington, where
                                   the ENSEMBLE (as SPECTATORS) are
                                   gathered for the inauguration of
                                   Donald Trump. Sat among them,
                                   CONWAY, ERIC, IVANKA, JUNIOR,
                                   and SEAN SPICER.

                                   The NARRATOR enters to stand at
                                   the glass podium front center.

                           NARRATOR
The twentieth day of the year's first month, a day which
many in the world hopes will end shortly before lunch. For
today is the day that judgment will fall. Today is the day
that parents will call to tell their children they love
them all.

On Capitol Hill in Washington DC, a breeze blows slowly
over all that's to be.
                           (MORE)

                                                  (CONTINUED)

NARRATOR (CONT'D)

And as he prepares to take his spot among those who before
him's legacies he'll soon work to rot, friends of his
gather among those foes who still matter. While out in the
crowds, thousands now stand to shout to him cheers, while
walking the streets millions more prepare to scream leers.
Three million votes behind, but that's never a fact his
supporters will mind, for all they want to see is their new
president claiming to be making them free.

Celebration will follow for all those who for Donald they
did vote, while a drive to inspire change will fill many
more of those who begin to take note.

An inauguration of unity is what many will claim, but days
will follow where Barack Obama is still given the blame.

And so as Trump and Pence to this spot they make their way,
it's time to begin the ceremony that will keep decency at
bay.

MICHELLE (OFF)

Barack, hurry up. You don't want to miss it.

BILL, CLINTON, and MICHELLE
enter.

CLINTON

I wouldn't be so sure about that.

MICHELLE

Barack.

OBAMA enters and joins them.

OBAMA

Oh... my... god...

CLINTON

Hey, where are the Carters?

MICHELLE

They called this morning and said their train has been
canceled.

(CONTINUED)

                          CLINTON
Dang it. Why didn't we think of that?

                          BILL
What about the Bushes? I was hoping to catch up with W.

                          MICHELLE
He accidentally booked his flights to the wrong Washington.

                          OBAMA
Oh... my... god...

                                   The four of them take their
                                   seats among the crowd.

                          NARRATOR
And now, please find something to hold on to as we welcome
President-Elect, Donald Trump, and Vice-President-Elect,
Mike Pence.

                                   PENCE and TRUMP enter.

                          TRUMP
Mike Pence, why is your wife not here to watch you today?

                          PENCE
Oh, Mother said she had an appointment with her doctor
scheduled for today.

                          TRUMP
What a coincidence. Mary said the same thing to me.

                          PENCE
Who is Mary, sir?

                          TRUMP
Number three.

                                   Together, they make their way
                                   towards the podium and shake
                                   hands with the NARRATOR.

                                                      (CONTINUED)

>   CLINTON hands the NARRATOR a
>   bottle of hand sanitizer.

                         CLINTON
Here, take this.

>   The NARRATOR cleans their hands
>   then hands the bottle back.

                         NARRATOR
Thank you.

                         CLINTON
No problem. Just remember to vote for me in four years. Or
just remember me... please remember me.

                         NARRATOR
                    (to PENCE and TRUMP)
Mister Trump. Mister Pence. If you're both ready, we'll get
started.

                         TRUMP
Before we begin, I do not like the Bible. I prefer people
named Jesus who do not get crucified, and so I have a
different book to swear on.

>   He brings a book from his pocket
>   and shows it to the audience.

                         TRUMP
It is a great book. Such a fantastic read. It is called --

                         NARRATOR
The Art of the Deal by Donald J. Trump.

                         TRUMP
Available now from the failing Amazon dot com, which I hear
is owned by the failing Washington Post loser.

                         PENCE
Such a strong statement, sir.

                         TRUMP
Thank you, Mike Pence.

                                              (CONTINUED)

CONTINUED:

> The NARRATOR gestures towards
> the book.

                    NARRATOR
Mister Pence, would you mind?

> PENCE takes the book and holds
> it for TRUMP to place his hand
> upon.

                    NARRATOR
                (to audience)
Ladies, gentlemen, and Bill Clinton. We are gathered here
today to mourn the loss of democracy, compassion, decency,
and, most importantly of all, style in the White House.

                    TRUMP
It is going to be so great.

                    NARRATOR
We'll begin with the President-Elect.
                (to TRUMP)
Donald Jenius Trump, do you solemnly swear that you will
faithlessly embarrass your country on the world stage,
insult and alienate allies, and to the best of your
ability, completely ignore the Constitution of the United
States?

                    TRUMP
So help me, Comrade Vladimir Putin.

                    NARRATOR
Then if nobody has any objections...

> CLINTON stands, but BILL pulls
> her down.

                    CLINTON
I've got a few.

                    NARRATOR
Then I do now declare you to be...

                                                (CONTINUED)

                          OBAMA
Oh... my... god...

                          NARRATOR
The President of the United States.

                          OBAMA
Wait.

                              Everyone on stage watches as
                              OBAMA stands and makes his way
                              to the podium.

                          OBAMA
If you wouldn't mind, Narrator, I would like to say...
something.

                          NARRATOR
Please go ahead.

                          OBAMA
Thank you.

                              The NARRATOR steps to the side
                              as OBAMA begins to address the
                              audience.

                          OBAMA
Now a lot of people have asked me, ever since the election,
about what I think of the fact that this suntanned turd...
is going to become the President of the United States... I
have not given an answer to that inquiry before, but today,
I am going to give you one... Because the answer is really
quite simple... Let me tell you now that the answer is
yes... yes I do like piña coladas, and I also enjoy...
getting caught in the rain.

                              He rips off his pants to reveal
                              a pair of Hawaiian shorts.

                          OBAMA
                      (to the NARRATOR)
Narrator, my sunglasses if you please.

                                                    (CONTINUED)

CONTINUED:

                        The NARRATOR takes a pair of
                        sunglasses from their pocket and
                        hands them over.

                          OBAMA
I'm not running things anymore, and that means none of this
crap... is my responsibility.
                    (to MICHELLE)
Michelle.

                        MICHELLE stands and joins him.

                          OBAMA
We're off to Tahiti to go jet-skiing. Obamas out.

                        Hand in hand, they both exit. A
                        beat follows.

                          CLINTON
Well, that was some weird shit.

                        Beat.

                          TRUMP
Can we move on to Mike Pence now?

                        PENCE hands TRUMP the book, who
                        then holds it for him to place
                        his hand upon.

                          NARRATOR
Of course.
                    (to PENCE)
Michael Richard Pence, do you solemnly swear that you will
accept your fate of being forever remembered by history as
responsible for all of the terrible things that Donald
Trump goes on to do, to not fulfill a single one of your
responsibilities to ensure that the President follows the
law, and to waste thousands of dollars by storming out
sports events that you never wanted to go to in the first
place?

                          PENCE
I do.

                                              (CONTINUED)

PERFORMANCE LICENSE EDITION   LICENSE # _ _ _ _ _ _ _ _

CONTINUED:

                         NARRATOR
Then I do declare you to be the Vice-President.

                              All (except CLINTON and the
                              NARRATOR) begin to applaud.

                              Noticing BILL clapping, CLINTON
                              moves his hands down.

                         BILL
Sorry, Hillary. I just find it emotional.

                         CLINTON
I need to find a bar.

                         NARRATOR
I need to join you.

                              CLINTON and the NARRATOR exit as
                              TRUMP takes to the podium.

                         TRUMP
Well, Narrator, thank you very much. President Obama, I do
not know where he has gone. I guess he has to run to the
airport before his visa expires. Also, I would also like to
thank all of those great patriotic Americans who voted for
me.
                         (beat)
Today is a very special day because today we are taking
such great and fantastic power away from Washington, a man
who I hear is overrated, and giving it to Russia.

Throughout this brutal election campaign, ordinary American
voters have told me that they want great things like
schools, they want lots of schools, and also safe
neighborhoods. I have also been told that small business
owners want a strong economy and skilled people to work for
them. But in life, you do not always get what you want. If
they wanted those things, then they should have voted for
Crooked Hillary Clinton.

What I am going to do is make America great again. And to
do this, trust me, such fantastic things will be happening.
                         (MORE)

                                                   (CONTINUED)

TRUMPED: AN ALTERNATIVE MUSICAL
PART ONE (ACT I & ACT II)
CONTINUED:

TRUMP (CONT'D)

Everything is going to be so great that you will not even
know that it is great. That is how great it is going to be.

There will be lots of jobs. We are going to create so many
jobs for people like lawyers. So many lawyers, and also
comedians. There is going to be so many lawyers and so many
comedians, that it is going to be like an N-B-C production
office in the year two thousand and ten.
Most importantly of all, I am going to give this country
what it really needs. We are going to have, prepare for
your minds to be blown, a space force. We are going to have
rockets, fast rockets that go whoosh. Also, we will have
some that go wheeee.

For the true patriots of this country, we are also going to
have such a great display of fireworks above our cities on
our Independence Day, June fifth, courtesy of little rocket
man and North Korea.

I know a lot of people are worried right now about the
safety and the security of your family, but to you, I ask a
question, in the event of a nuclear war, would it not be
cool to become a super hero?
                    (beat)
And now, I am going to hand over to Mike Pence.

                         TRUMP stands back as PENCE takes
                         to the podium.

                    PENCE
Well, what are we all standing around for? This is supposed
to be a party. Comrades, let's dance.

ACT II, SCENE SEVEN | THE INAUGURATION PARTY

                         A BALLROOM where in an instant
                         the dress of those on stage has
                         changed to attire of distinctly
                         Russian origin. Equally as
                         Russian is the music now filling
                         the stage.

                                        (CONTINUED)

>   While the ENSEMBLE and others
>   remain on stage, PENCE and TRUMP
>   have disappeared.

                         CONWAY
Comrades, please welcome the President and Vice-President.

>   Synchronized, PENCE and TRUMP
>   return and begin to dance
>   Barynya center stage. Circled
>   around them, their guests clap
>   and cheer as they watch.
>
>   After a short time, PENCE and
>   TRUMP take a bow together and
>   then move to the side to allow
>   CONWAY and SPICER to take the
>   floor together.
>
>   Again, those around them clap
>   and cheer for a short while
>   until PENCE and TRUMP join them,
>   and all four dance together.
>   As the music begins to slow, the
>   dancing stops, and all on stage
>   stand arm in arm to sing.

                    ENSEMBLE (EXCEPT TRUMP)
                         (drunkenly)
/DONALD TRUMP IS OUR PRESIDENT, DONALD TRUMP IS OUR MAN. WE
ALL LOVE DONALD TRUMP, HE'S OUR MAN, DONALD TRUMP IS OUR
MAN. HEY!/

>   Silence, and then the music
>   builds once more for ERIC,
>   IVANKA, and JUNIOR to now take
>   center stage.
>
>   While IVANKA and JUNIOR dance
>   synchronized, however, ERIC
>   stands watching them both
>   confused until eventually he
>   drops the floor and begins to
>   spin himself around.

                                              (CONTINUED)

> As the three of them move to the
> side, next to take the floor is
> a topless PUTIN, who enters by
> cartwheeling from the wings
> before performing a solo.

> Finally, as PUTIN finishes, the
> entire stage begins to dance
> together until abruptly, the
> music stops, and the stage
> clears to leave BILL on his own.

                    BILL
I am going to be in so much trouble if Hillary finds out
that I stayed for the party.

ACT II, SCENE EIGHT | THE FIRST PRESS BRIEFING

> The WHITE HOUSE PRESS BRIEFING
> ROOM where the ENSEMBLE (as
> PRESS) sit facing a podium,
> behind which, the NARRATOR
> stands.

                  NARRATOR
With the inauguration over and the party at an end --

> SPICER enters and begins to push
> the NARRATOR away.

                   SPICER
Hey, hey, no. Not your place. Listen here, Narrator person,
I don't know who you are or what you're doing here, but
this is not your show, do you understand? Now get off this
stage before I strangle you with the piece of gum I'm
chewing right now.

> After pushing the NARRATOR
> offstage, he takes his place at
> the podium.

                                            (CONTINUED)

                              SPICER
Okay, now I want all of you son's of bitches to listen up,
so I don't have to repeat myself. First up, it's item
number one, I have a hangover after the inauguration party
last night. It's what big boys and big girls get after they
drink alcohol. You'll all learn about that one day.

                              PRESS #1
Like the morning after impeachment.

                              SPICER
Right, I heard that. You, what's your name?

                              PRESS #1
Ayma.

                              SPICER
That should be Ayma, sir. Do you understand that? Let's try
it again, what's your name?

                              PRESS #1
Ayma, sir.

                              SPICER
Good, and what's your second name?

                              PRESS #1
Moron.

                              SPICER
Ayma Moron.

                         The ENSEMBLE laugh.

                              SPICER
Oh, right, I get it. It's a joke. It's joke around with
Spicy day, is it? Well, not on my watch. See me in my
office at the end of the day. I'm also taking ten points
away from C-N-N house for your pathetic attempt to be the
joker in the group.

                              PRESS #2
C-N-N house? Sean, this isn't some sort of school for
magic.

                                                    (CONTINUED)

                              SPICER
Well, you all could have fooled me, that's for sure. I read
all of your reports on the inauguration this morning, and
nearly all of you just conjured up the size of the crowd.
Staying with this, we come to item number two. I'm not
mentioning any names, okay, but I am looking at you when I
say this New York Times. You can't just lie about the
figures to make the President look bad. You were all there,
and you all saw the billions --

                            PRESS #3
Billions, Sean?

                              SPICER
Okay, millions then. Happy now? You all saw the millions of
people who came out to watch the President.

                            PRESS #4
Sean, most of them were protesters.

                              SPICER
Okay, but tell me this, would they have been there if it
wasn't for the President.

                            PRESS #4
They were protesting the President.

                              SPICER
But would they have been protesting the President if it
wasn't his inauguration? Would they have been protesting
Hillary Clinton?

                            PRESS #4
No, they would have been there to celebrate instead.

                              SPICER
Okay, that... that is sort of my point. Here's what's going
to happen, all of you are going to go and write me a new
draft of your inauguration reports using the correct crowd
size figures as homework, even you The Washington Post. I
want all of them on my desk first thing tomorrow, or I will
write home to your parents.

                              PRESS #5 raises their hand.

                                                  (CONTINUED)

                         SPICER
Yes, you from Fox News.

                         PRESS #5
Master Hannity sent an apple for me to give you, sir.

                         SPICER
Well, you can tell Sean Hannity that I don't like apples. I
don't go within three feet of any fruit. But it's a nice
gesture, and so I'll tell you what, at recess, you can have
the first choice of toy to play with.

                         PRESS #2
Sean --

                         SPICER
What?

                         PRESS #2
Are you some sort of joke?

                         SPICER
Stop asking questions. The next person who asks me a
question can stand outside until we're done. Okay, we move
on now to item number three. For the stupid among you,
which is all of you, that is one less than four, but one
more than two. It says here that the President will later
today walk from the White House Residence across to the
Oval Office. I don't know what that is so don't ask.
Perhaps it's an office in some sort of Oval shape? I don't
know. Perhaps you can all Google it. To sign some executive
orders with Paul Ryan and Mitch McConnell.

                         PRESS #6
Sean, what will these executive orders be about?

                         SPICER
What did I just tell you all about asking questions? I'm
marking your name down.
                    (beat)
Okay, so it says here that there will be multiple, that
means more than one, executive orders signed that will be
great in nature. So there are some great things going to be
happening, report that, that is your news.
                       (MORE)
                                              (CONTINUED)

PERFORMANCE LICENSE EDITION   LICENSE # _ _ _ _ _ _ _ _

CONTINUED:

                         SPICER (CONT'D)
Oh, and it also says that the President will be ordering
people to stop laughing at Mitch McConnell.
                         (beat)
Now during this walk to this circular shaped office, the
President will be joined by his third lady, and I am told
that she will be wearing a long white robe topped with a
wizard-like hat... no, wait, that's going to be the
President. It says Melania will be wearing a bag over her
head because she's embarrassed to be seen with her husband.

                         PRESS #1
Can we report that?

                         SPICER
No. You're all going to report this instead. The First
Lady, Melania Trump, loves... Why aren't you all writing
this down? Get writing before I write it on your faces
using C-N-N's blood for ink.

                    They all begin writing.

                         SPICER
Okay, the First Lady, Melania Trump, loves the President,
that's Donald Trump, very much. The two of them regularly,
and there's a note here that says regularly is at least
three times a week, make love together in the evenings.
Except for the President who makes love five times a week.

                         There's a flash as someone takes
                         a photo.

                         SPICER
Okay, which of you little assholes is taking photos? Was it
you, Washington Post?

                         PRESS #3
My editor asked me to get a photo because you're not
allowing cameras in here.

                         SPICER
Oh, and I suppose that you think you're just going to print
some photo of me in your newspaper with a caption about the
news? Something like this here.
                    (checking his notes)
                         (MORE)

                                             (CONTINUED)

CONTINUED:
SPICER (CONT'D)
Giant Weiner, Sean Spicer, confirms that the President is
not lacking down there.
(beat)
I don't want to see another camera. No more photos. Believe
it or not, some of us in this administration don't actually
photograph too well. I'm not mentioning names, but you all
know I'm on about Steve Bannon. And then there's Stephen
Miller, he doesn't photograph at all.

PRESS #3
Past administrations have always allowed these briefings to
be broadcast so they can be open to the people.

SPICER
This is not a past administration, is it? This is Spicer's
time, and what I say goes. It works like this. The
President decides what the news is, and then he tells me,
Sean Spicer. I then tell all of you what the news is, and
then you go and dumb it down for your readers and your
viewers so that they know what the news is.

PRESS #3
What is the news today?

SPICER
I haven't had the chance to discuss it with the President
yet.

PRESS #1
Sean, did you just call all of our readers and viewers dumb
right now? They are all voters.

SPICER
Of course, I'm calling them dumb. Three million more of
them voted illegally for Hillary Clinton rather than our
President, and for some reason, they all decided to vote in
California. I'm not sure what's going on there, but I would
say that's pretty dumb C-N-N.

PRESS #4
Can we quote you on that, Sean?

(CONTINUED)

PERFORMANCE LICENSE EDITION   LICENSE # _ _ _ _ _ _ _ _

                         SPICER
                    (mocking at first)
"Can we quote you on that, Sean?" How about I quote you on
your dying words as I strangle you with your iPhone
charger? And don't try to pretend you don't all have
iPhones, okay? I know that you liberal fake news people all
use Apple stuff. Siri told me.

                         PRESS #1
Sean, I really think that the administration has a duty to
show people what they're doing. It's only right that you
allow cameras in here.

                         SPICER
Well in here it's not what you think that matters. I decide
what happens, the President decides what I decide what
happens, and Comrade Vladimir Putin decides what the
President decides what I decide what happens. It is simple.

                         PRESS #1
                      (standing)
I'm sorry, but I think we all have a duty to the people
here. Who's with me?

                         PRESS #4
                      (standing)
She's right.

                         PRESS #3
                      (standing)
I don't think we should do any more reporting until the
cameras are turned back on.

                         PRESS #2
                      (standing)
I think it's time to boycott Sean Spicer.

                              They all stand, except for PRESS
                              #5.

                         SPICER
Oh really? So you're all going to be principled? You're all
going to rally together to stand up to this administration
and make a point?

                                             (CONTINUED)

                         Beat, and they all sit.

                         PRESS #4
Actually, I'm going to leave it to someone else.

                         PRESS #1
I'm sure there are protesters working on this stuff.

                         SPICER
That's what I thought. Okay, we come to item number four
now. The President will, that means he is going to, in a
few days time be hosting a woman from Germany who goes by
the name of... I think it's angled moo-cow.

                         PRESS #2
Sean, do you mean Angela Merkel, the Chancellor of Germany?

                         SPICER
I mean what I said. Don't make me repeat myself.

                         He checks his notes.

                         SPICER
Actually, now that I look at it, it might be Angle --

                         PRESS #2
Angela Merkel?

                         SPICER
Yes, that. Alright, none of you remember that I got that
name wrong, okay. You, C-N-N, are you remembering? I can
see you remembering right now.
                    (beat)
Okay, I think we're done here now. There are some minor
things about banning an entire religion and abolishing all
forms of healthcare, but the details aren't important.

                         He goes to leave as a mumble
                         breaks out.

                         PRESS #3
Banning a religion?

                                                      (CONTINUED)
PERFORMANCE LICENSE EDITION   LICENSE # _ _ _ _ _ _ _ _

PRESS #2
Abolishing healthcare? We need more information than that.

SPICER
Okay, I want fingers on lips.

PRESS #1
What?

SPICER
You heard me, fingers on lips.

> Confused, they do as they're
> told.

SPICER
Are you not all journalists in here?

> They nod.

SPICER
Good, then look up the news and work it out for yourselves.
I'm going for a lie-down.

ACT II, SCENE NINE | MERKEL VISITS THE WHITE HOUSE

> Remaining in the WHITE HOUSE
> PRESS BRIEFING ROOM where the
> ENSEMBLE (as PRESS) remain on
> stage, now in front of two
> podiums that stand between a
> United States flag and a German
> flag.

NARRATOR
(entering)
And so as Spicer said in the days ahead, Merkel flew to
meet with the orange guy who when first told he had won
simply said WHO!?. The first world leader to make the trip,
why? Every other had suddenly developed an injury, a four-
year dip. No one wanted to be the first to meet with their
new counterpart who was now the worst.
(MORE)

(CONTINUED)

CONTINUED:

                    NARRATOR (CONT'D)
But at the end of the first of her trips, multiple days
filled with multiple blips, a duty she knows she has does
Angela, to straight out the President and to keep her hands
triangular.

                        PRESS #2
Does anyone else feel like we've been here for days?

                        NARRATOR
Ladies, gentlemen, and Fox News of the White House Press
Pool, I present to you the Chancellor of Germany, Angela
Merkel, and President Donald J. Trump.

                              ANGELA MERKEL and TRUMP enter
                              and take their places behind the
                              podiums.

                        TRUMP
Today, I am honored to welcome European President Angel
Murky to the White House.

                              MERKEL begins to drink from a
                              glass of water.

                        TRUMP
I have enjoyed speaking to her today, and I am sure that
she has greatly enjoyed speaking to me too, okay folks.

                              MERKEL spits out her water.

                        MERKEL
I apologize.

                        TRUMP
                    (ignoring MERKEL)
We have a great relationship, and let me tell you, there
has never been a time when our country has had more in
common with Germany.
                    (beat)
I would like now to hand over to Missus Merkel.
                    (to MERKEL)
Chancellor, thank you.

                                        (CONTINUED)

MERKEL
Narrator, can you translate?

The NARRATOR nods.

MERKEL
Thank you.

She takes a deep breath.

MERKEL
Danke schön, so genannt Herr Präsident.

NARRATOR
Thank you very much, so-called Mister President.

TRUMP pulls out his phone and
begins to play a game on it.

MERKEL
Das ist alo der weg, den sie gewählt haben, Amerika?

NARRATOR
So this is the path you chose America?

MERKEL
Sie haben sich entschieden, den Fanta Fascist zu wählen.

NARRATOR
You have decided to elect the Fanta Fascist.

MERKEL
Ein wörtlicher großer käse.

NARRATOR
A literal big cheese.

MERKEL
Ein butterbefeuerter, sonnengebräunter xenophobie mit
händed in der größe von kinderhandschuhen.

NARRATOR
A butter-friend, sun-tanned xenophone with hands the size
of children's mittens.

(CONTINUED)

                         MERKEL
Der räuberische rassist des vierten reiches.

                         NARRATOR
The Rapacious Racist of the Fourth Reich.

                         MERKEL
Was zum verdammten wort hast du gedacht, Amerika?

                         NARRATOR
What the naughty word were you thinking, America?

                         MERKEL
Es ist als ob sie zweitausendsechzehn modell brandneue B-M-
W genhandelt haben.

                         NARRATOR
It's as though you traded in brand new two thousand and
sixteen model B-M-W.

                         MERKEL
In glattem schwarz.

                         NARRATOR
In smooth black.

                         MERKEL
Für neunzehnachtunddreißig Volkswagen Käfer in der sonne
orange.

                         NARRATOR
For nineteen thirty-eight Volkswagen Beetle in sunshine
orange.

                         MERKEL
Ernsthaft, der mann ist so dumm, der einzige grund warum er
keinen atomkrieg begonnen hat ist dass er den startcode
nicht buchstabieren kann.

                         NARRATOR
Seriously, the man is so stupid, the only reason he hasn't
started a nuclear war is that he can't spell the launch
codes.

                                              (CONTINUED)

                         MERKEL
Sie sind nur eins, zwei, drei, vier, ich erkläre einen
atomkrieg.

                         NARRATOR
They're only one, two, three, four, I declare a nuclear
war.

                         MERKEL
Barack hat es mir gesagt.

                         NARRATOR

Barack told me.

                         MERKEL
                       (with lust)
Oh Barack, vie sehr vermisse ich ihn. Sicher, ich wusste
dass er nicht mehr Präsident sein konnte, aber ich dachte
Hillary würde in der lage sein mit ihm kaffee zu kochen um
über alte zeiten zu reden.

                         NARRATOR
Oh Barack, how I miss him so much. Sure, I knew he couldn't
be president anymore, but I thought that Hillary could set
up coffee with him so we could talk about old times.

                         MERKEL
Obwohl er vielleicht mehr zeit hat, mich zu besuchen. Ich
sagte ihm, Barack, wenn du jemals in Berlin bist, komm und
sag hallo und ich werde dich herumführen. Ich kenne die
besten plätze, wo wir uns hinsetzen und zu mittag essen
können, während die sonne untergeht, während wir uns über
wechselkursmechanismen und außenpolitik im Nahen Osten
unterhalten.

                         NARRATOR
Although he may...
                       (beat, then to MERKEL)
Sorry, could I have that slower?

                         MERKEL
Obwohl er vielleicht mehr zeit hat, mich zu besuchen.

                                              (CONTINUED)

CONTINUED:

>   NARRATOR
> Although he may have more time to visit me.

>   MERKEL
> Ich sagte ihm, Barack, wenn du jemals in Berlin bist, komm
> und sag hallo und ich werde dich herumführen.

>   NARRATOR
> I told him, Barack, if you're ever in Berlin, come and say
> hello and I'll show you around.

>   MERKEL
> Ich kenne die besten plätze, wo wir uns hinsetzen und zu
> mittag essen können, während die sonne untergeht, während
> wir uns über wechselkursmechanismen und außenpolitik im
> Nahen Osten unterhalten.

>   NARRATOR
> I know the best places where we can sit down and have lunch
> while the sun goes down as we talk about foreign exchange
> mechanisms and our policies in the Middle East.

>   MERKEL
> Wir hätten so viel Spaß zusammen haben können. Nicht wie
> Honky Honky Spaß, nein, ich meine, ha ha, Lachen Sie laut L-
> O-L Spaß. ROFL.

>   NARRATOR
> We could have had so much fun together. Not like Honky
> Honky fun, no, I mean, ha ha, laugh loud L-O-L fun. ROFL.

>   MERKEL
> Aber jetzt muss ich mit Trumpelstiltskin über handelsregeln
> reden.

>   NARRATOR
> But now I've to discuss trade rules with Trumpelstiltskin.

>   MERKEL
> Ich habe neulich mit Justin Trudeau telefoniert. Theresa
> May denkt nicht viel von ihm, aber ich denke, dass er ein
> schöner mann ist. Seine arme sind so stark und er hat ein
> gesicht, das mich heiß und verschwitzt macht.

                                                 (CONTINUED)
PERFORMANCE LICENSE EDITION   LICENSE # _ _ _ _ _ _ _

                    NARRATOR
I spoke to Justin Trudeau the other day. Theresa May does
not think much of him, bit I think he is a handsome man.
His arms are so strong and he has a face that makes me all
hot and sweaty.

                    MERKEL
Wie auch immer, er sagte, dass er darüber nachdachte,
Donald auf dem G-7—Gipfel im nächsten Jahr den falschen
platz zu nennen, damit wir ihn nicht ertagen mussten.

                    NARRATOR
Anyway, he said that he's considering giving Donald the
wrong location of the G-7 summit next year so we don't have
to endure him.

                    MERKEL
Es wäre immer so ein lustiger witz.

                    NARRATOR
It would be such a fun joke.

                    MERKEL
Ich schätze, ich sollte jetzt der mächtigen mango
zurückgeben, damit er euch alle noch mehr belügen kann.

                    NARRATOR
Well, I guess I should hand back over to the mighty mango
so he can lie to you some more.

                    MERKEL
P-S das pipi ist echt. Ich habe es gesehen.

                    NARRATOR
P-S the pee-pee tape is real. I've seen it.

                    MERKEL
Mister President, over to you.

                              TRUMP remains focussed on his
                              phone.

                    NARRATOR
Mister Trump, sir.

                                             (CONTINUED)

                          TRUMP
                      (looking up)
Oh, is the woman done now? I was playing golf on my phone.
I discovered that if I change the screen settings, I can
make the little man in the game look as orange as me.

                          MERKEL
Er hat auch die gleichen Hände wie du, du komplett
verdammter trottel.

                          NARRATOR
He also has the same size hands as you, you --

                          MERKEL
Actually, don't translate the rest of that. I need a drink
now.

                    She exits.

                          TRUMP
Does that mean I can go too? I want to watch the end of Fox
and Friends while my McMuffin is still warm.

                              The NARRATOR nods and TRUMP and
                              the ENSEMBLE exit.

ACT II, SCENE TEN | COOPER & CONWAY

                              The CNN STUDIO, where COOPER is
                              halfway through interviewing
                              (and arguing with) CONWAY on his
                              show.

                          NARRATOR
It's a fact that in any ordinary circumstances, the meeting
of two world leaders would be the day's news, but it also
remains that Donald J. Trump's opinion of what truly
matters are very different views. And so rather than to
praise the trade the United States from Germany hopes to
graze, he sends on Kellyanne Conway live to defend his
crowd size and popularly dive.

                    The NARRATOR exits.

                                              (CONTINUED)

TRUMPED: AN ALTERNATIVE MUSICAL
PART ONE (ACT I & ACT II)

CONTINUED:

                         COOPER
I'm just not sure that you actually understand, Kellyanne.
The role of the media and the press is to report the facts,
not to make the President look good.

                         CONWAY
I'm not sure that you're getting it, Anderson. The
President is good, and that's why what he says are the
facts. Why are you seeing to discredit the President?

                         COOPER
I'm not seeking to discredit the President. The President
is discrediting himself, and you're helping him to do that.

                         CONWAY
Well, I don't agree with that. You and the other members of
the liberal mainstream media have been lying about the size
of the inauguration crowd size for days now.

                         COOPER
Why are we back to the crowd size?

                         CONWAY
Do you know how many times Hillary Clinton visited places
like Bowling Green during the election? That small town is
the location of one of this country's worst-ever massacres,
and she didn't go to pay her respects once.

                         COOPER
Kellyanne, what are you on about? There's never been a
massacre in a place called Bowling Green.

                         CONWAY
Okay, it is very disrespectful for you to pretend that
nothing happened, Anderson. But I really don't expect
anything else from C-N-N because none of you care about
lives being lost in Republican states.

                         COOPER
When you're failing to defend yourself, you can't just
change the subject to a made-up massacre and then accuse an
entire network of being disrespectful because no one else
has heard of it.

                                                  (CONTINUED)

                         CONWAY
Actually yes I can do that, Anderson.

                         COOPER
You were on about crowd sizes, I believe?

                         CONWAY
You see, Anderson? It isn't me that's bringing up the
subject of crowd sizes, it's you.

                         COOPER
No, you brought it up and then tried to distract from it by
making something else up.

                         CONWAY
Why do you and C-N-N keep refusing to accept how many
people turned out to celebrate President Trump's
inauguration?

                         COOPER
We prefer to consider the facts, and all of the live
footage from the day shows that turnout was significantly
lower than any previous inauguration.

                         CONWAY
That's not true, and you know it, Anderson. Our Press
Secretary, Sean Spicer, has spent a lot of time trying to
explain the facts to your reporter at the White House, so
how can you still continue to get it wrong?

                         COOPER
Sean Spicer hid in the bushes outside our reporter's house
all night so that he could threaten them with a twig when
they left the next morning.

                         CONWAY
Sure, but after that, he pointed out that millions of
people turned out to see the President.

                         COOPER
Then he was lying.

                         CONWAY
No, he wasn't lying.

                                              (CONTINUED)

                         COOPER
Then what was he doing? Every single factual source proves
that what he was claiming is false.

                         CONWAY
He was giving alternative facts.

                         COOPER
I'm sorry?

                         CONWAY
Sean Spicer was giving alternative facts.

                    COOPER begins to laugh.

                         COOPER
I didn't have any trouble hearing you, Kellyanne.

                         CONWAY
There's no need to laugh, Anderson. You're supposed to be a
professional.

                         COOPER
I don't even know what to say.

                    He laughs harder.

                         CONWAY
That's okay. I know that you understand the truth now.

                         COOPER
It's not that, it's just stupid. It's so stupid.

                         CONWAY
I can wait until you're done. I'm more mature than this,
and I'm going to be the bigger person.

                    COOPER laughs harder still.

                         COOPER
You're on here representing the President of the United
States. What's going on?

                                              (CONTINUED)

> Laughing even harder, he falls
> off his chair onto the floor.

COOPER

How can any of this be happening?

> The NARRATOR enters and rushes
> to COOPER'S side.

NARRATOR

Anderson, speak to me, are you okay? Speak to me.

COOPER

Everything is just so stupid.

NARRATOR
(shouting out)

We need help here.

> The NARRATOR exits before
> rushing back with a first aid
> kit, but as they approach COOPER
> again, they are rugby tackled by
> PAUL RYAN, who enters at speed.

RYAN
(to the NARRATOR)

Let me tell you what the problem is here. You want to help
Anderson Cooper, but Anderson Cooper hasn't paid for his
healthcare. Now not only has he collapsed, but he's going
to get worse if you do nothing. We can fix this problem
with a three-pronged approach. Number one, someone is going
to pay for his healthcare. Number two, you are going to
treat him. Number three, I am going to pass a law that bans
all mirrors, so that I never have to look at myself again.

> RYAN release the NARRATOR as
> they hand him a bundle of bills
> from their pocket.

RYAN

I don't want to get into the specifics of what just
happened.

(CONTINUED)

                        He exits as the NARRATOR helps
                        COOPER back onto his chair.

                COOPER
I think that it's time for us to take a commercial break
right now. Thank you, Kellyanne Conway, for joining me.

                        The NARRATOR exits as CONWAY
                        pulls out her phone and begins
                        to dial a number.

                CONWAY
You know, Anderson, I really think that we're going to have
to rethink our relationship.

                COOPER
What relationship? I don't want to rethink any relationship
with you. We don't have one, and I want to keep it that
way.

                CONWAY
I'll talk to you after I've called my husband.

                        She puts the phone to her ear.

                CONWAY
              (on phone)
Hey George. Yes, I've just finished my interview with
Anderson Cooper, and I should be home soon. We can have
that special meal we've been planning tonight.
              (beat)
You know Anderson, he's the one that looks like the love
child of Mike Pence's hair and Andy from Toy Story.

                        A PRODUCTION ASSISTANT enters
                        and hands COOPER a memo before
                        exiting.

                COOPER
You might want to hold your plans, Kellyanne.

                CONWAY
What?

                              (CONTINUED)

PERFORMANCE LICENSE EDITION   LICENSE # _ _ _ _ _ _ _ _

CONTINUED:

COOPER
And we're live in three, two, one... Hello, and welcome
back to Anderson Cooper three-sixty with me, Anderson
Cooper. Still with me, senior aide to the President,
Kellyanne Conway, who I hope can give us her take on some
breaking news just in. F-B-I director James Comey has, in
the past few minutes, announced that he will be launching a
formal investigation into possible collusion between the
Trump campaign and the Russian Government. Kellyanne...

CONWAY
(on phone)
George, I'm going to have to call you back.

ACT II, SCENE ELEVEN | THE WHITE HOUSE DAY CARE CENTER

                              A WHITE HOUSE OFFICE where ERIC,
                              KUSHNER, and TRUMP stand holding
                              hands in a circle along with a
                              DAY CARE ASSISTANT.

NARRATOR
(entering)
With the candlelit dinner at home now to be eaten by George
Conway alone, Kellyanne sets off to the Whitehouse with
haste, the last words from Cooper still leaving a
particularly bad taste. Her boss is now the subject of
multiple questions, and she can't help but worry that to
answer them exactly what will be his suggestions.

But while with ideas of her own in mind she travels, ahead
Donald Trump is ensuring already that any plan just
unravels. For rather than calling his advisors to talk, he
calls in James Comey to tell him to walk. The F-B-I
Director on the spot fired. A move which only by idiots can
ever be admired.

But rather than let just the one man go, where to stop
firing, the President does not know. From an agency head,
and a chief of staff too, each one distracting from the
news that does brew.
(MORE)

(CONTINUED)

CONTINUED:
                         NARRATOR (CONT'D)
But how many more departures can he get away with? All why
trying to keep on the truth, his solid gold lid.

                    The NARRATOR exits.

                    DAY CARE ASSISTANT
Okay, so are we all ready to take it from the top again?
One, two, three...

               TRUMP/ ERIC/ DAY CARE ASSISTANT
/YOU PUT THE RACIST IN, THE RACIST OUT, YOU PUT A RACIST
BACK IN AND DENY WHAT IT'S ABOUT. WHEN THE PRESS ASK
QUESTIONS YOU IGNORE THEM ALL, THAT'S WHAT IT'S ALL ABOUT./

                    DAY CARE ASSISTANT
Very good, Donald. I think you're the best here. Do you
want a verse of your own?

                         TRUMP
/I BROUGHT JAMES COMEY IN, TO MY OFFICE, AND I FIRED HIM, I
FIRED HIM, I TOLD HIM TO GET OUT. I FIRED HIM, AND THEN THE
LOSER RAN, HE SQUEALED LIKE A LITTLE MOUSE./

                    CONWAY enters.

                    DAY CARE ASSISTANT
And who is this joining us? It looks as though we have a
new face. Come in and introduce yourself to the group.

                         CONWAY
Oh, no, I'm not here to join in. I was told the President
was here, and I need to speak to him.

                    DAY CARE ASSISTANT
Well, don't take too long. We're going to start doing some
painting soon.

                    TRUMP approaches CONWAY.

                         TRUMP
What is it you want, Kellyanne Conway?

                                             (CONTINUED)
PERFORMANCE LICENSE EDITION   LICENSE # _ _ _ _ _ _ _ _

                         CONWAY
Just some dignity.
                    (beat)
Mister President, what is this place?

                         TRUMP
This is the White House day care center, Kellyanne Conway.

                         CONWAY
How come I've never heard of it before?

                         TRUMP
Why would you have? It is a secret group for top secret
agents. You have to be a big boy to be invited. We even
have codenames. I am Dusty Don, Sean Spicer usually comes,
and his codename is Bushmaster, Jared Kushner is the Silent
Stalker, and Eric Trump is --

                         CONWAY
Is he Eric, sir?

                         TRUMP
Do not be stupid. His codename is Evan.

                         CONWAY
Mister President, I need to speak to you about James Comey.

                         TRUMP
Do not worry about James Comey, Kellyanne Conway. He is
just a pastry chef at the F-B-I.

                         CONWAY
But Mister President, he's just announced that you and your
campaign is now under investigation for working with the
Russian Government.

                         TRUMP
I have already solved it. I fired him.

                         CONWAY lets out an involuntary
                         scream.

                         CONWAY
You fired him, sir?

                                        (CONTINUED)

                         TRUMP
I fired him.

                         CONWAY
Are you not worried that it's going to look like you're
obstructing justice?

                         TRUMP
What is that?

                         CONWAY
Oh, that's where someone's actions actively stop or delay
an investigation or justice being found.

                         TRUMP
I know what obstruction is, Kellyanne Conway. I mean, what
is justice?

                         CONWAY
I may not be the best person to tell you about that.

                         TRUMP
Either way, you are worrying without reason, Kellyanne
Conway.

                         CONWAY
What have you done, Sir?

                         TRUMP
I have fired loads of other people to distract from me
firing James Comey. Someone from the Office of Government
Ethics said it was inappropriate, and so I fired them too.

                         CONWAY
Mister President, this isn't going to look very good.

                         TRUMP
It will be okay. I have you to go and lie out there for me.

                    DAY CARE ASSISTANT
Donald, do you want to come and join us for Twinkle,
Twinkle, Little Star?

                                              (CONTINUED)

                          TRUMP
I have to go, Kellyanne Conway.

                                    TRUMP turns away as CONWAY
                                    reaches into her pocket for a
                                    bottle of medication that she
                                    begins to drink from.

                          TRUMP
                     (turning back)
One more thing, Kellyanne Conway. I have also just banned
all Muslims from entering the country.

                          CONWAY
                     (to herself, looking at the
                      bottle)
I'm going to need something stronger.

ACT II, SCENE TWELVE | THE SECOND PRESS BRIEFING

                                    The WHITE HOUSE PRESS BRIEFING
                                    ROOM and the ENSEMBLE (as PRESS,
                                    excluding PRESS #4) sit waiting
                                    in front of a podium.

                          NARRATOR
                     (entering)
Despite the best efforts to distract the President has made
to blur the facts, the press and the public believe still
wary for all of the President's answers feel too airy. For
them, there's something about James Comey's departures that
just doesn't add up, as though there's something being
hidden but ready to come up. And so it is that Sean Spicer
is sent to ensure that the reports of the press are all
equally as bent.

                                    SPICER enters and notices the
                                    NARRATOR.

                          SPICER
Hey, no. I've told you before. Get out!

                                              (CONTINUED)

>   The NARRATOR rushes to exit
>   before SPICER can reach them.

                    SPICER
                 (taking the podium)
Okay. You can shut up. You can shut up. You can shut up.
You can shut up. You especially can shut up, C-N-N, and New
York Times, you can shut up too.

Straight to it, item number one. You all seem to be having
some concerns about the recent staff changes around this
place, but let me tell you, you do not have any concerns,
is that clear? The President can fire who he wants when he
wants, okay.

                    PRESS #1
Sean, he just fired the F-B-I director while he was leading
an investigation into Russia's involvement with the
election and any help that the country offered to the Trump
campaign.

                    SPICER
Maybe you didn't understand it correctly, okay, or maybe
you're just really stupid, I don't know, but the President
did not fire James Comey because he was investigating him.
He fired James Comey because he was very mean to Hillary
Clinton about her emails.

                    PRESS #2
But the President was very mean to Hillary Clinton about
her emails. During the election, he got the crowds at all
of his rallies to shout that she should be locked up.

                    SPICER
Oh, so you finally say that he had crowds at his rallies
now and not a small gathering? Perhaps you can tell your
editor that, New York Times? But no, he didn't do that,
okay. You're making that up or just imagining it or
something.

                    PRESS #2
Sean, it's on tape.

                                        (CONTINUED)

TRUMPED: AN ALTERNATIVE MUSICAL
PART ONE (ACT I & ACT II)

165.

CONTINUED:

                         SPICER
Well, then it's an imaginary tape.

                         PRESS #6
The President also said himself in an interview with Sean
Hannity on Fox News the other day that he fired Comey
specifically because of the investigation and because he
refused to pledge his loyalty to him, something that is now
leading calls for a special prosecutor to be appointed not
only to take over the Russia investigation but also to look
at possible obstruction by the President.

                    They all begin taking notes.

                         PRESS #3
That's a good tip. I didn't have that.

                         SPICER
Seriously, you want to do this, M-S-N-B-C?

                         PRESS #6
I don't understand.

                         SPICER
Okay, you all call yourselves journalists. So how come as
so-called professionals, you're all believing everything
you see on the news?

                         PRESS #6
Sean --

                         SPICER
Just because the President said something on a television
show, it does not make it the truth. Are we clear on that?

                         PRESS #2
But what about the special prosecutor?

                         SPICER
Okay, no more questions. If there are any more questions,
then you'll all be in my office, and last time that
happened to one of you, you didn't leave the same.

                                              (CONTINUED)

PERFORMANCE LICENSE EDITION   LICENSE # _ _ _ _ _ _ _ _

                         PRESS #1
                        (shaking)
I... I saw things I can't unsee.

                         SPICER
There will be no special pro... damn it.

                         PRESS #6
Prosecutor?

                         SPICER
Yes. There won't be one of those. Period.
                        (beat)
Now, moving on to item number two. The Justice Department
will later today be announcing that they are appointing a
special pro... not again.

                         PRESS #6
Special Prosecutor?

                         SPICER
Yes, that. And I am told to tell you that this will be for
a period, okay.

                         PRESS #2
Sean --

                         SPICER
I said no questions, New York Times. We're going to move on
from item number two to item number three. The President
has appointed a new director of communications who is
starting today. It says here his name is... oh Jesus.

                         PRESS #6
Do you need help?

                         SPICER
No, I do not need help M-S-N-B-C. I can pronounce the name.
It's just, it's --

                    ANTHONY SCARAMUCCI enters.

                                                      (CONTINUED)

SCARAMUCCI

Me, Anthony Scaramucci! Hey, thanks for the introduction
there, Spicy, you little son of a bitch. How about we catch
up some time over my favorite dish, amuse-bouche? Or
perhaps we can catch a game, amuse-Mooch! Hey?

SPICER

Okay, that's it. I'm not doing this anymore. I sold the
last remaining bit of my soul and reputation for this job,
and I'm not prepared to now work with the abandoned twin of
some cartoon villain. Spicy is out.

                              SPICER exits as SCARAMUCCI takes
                              the podium.

SCARAMUCCI

Hey, what's that asshole's problem? I'm the Mooch! Everyone
loves the Mooch. Except for my wife, I've just heard she
wants a divorce. Mooch is sad. Poor Mooch.
                    (beat)
Hey, okay on to item number four. Steve Bannon sucks his
own cock.

PRESS #2

Can we quote you on that?

SCARAMUCCI

Yeah, why not? I'm the Mooch, and we all want it to be
true, don't we? Okay, item number five. The President has
fired Director of Communications, Anthony Scaramucci.
                    (waving)
Well, I'm off to go wrestle Reince Priebus. Hey, Mooch out!

                              SCARAMUCCI exits as SARAH
                              HUCKABEE SANDERS enters and
                              takes the podium.

HUCKABEE SANDERS

Hello there guys. I'm Sarah Huckabee Sanders, and I will be
taking over for Sean Spicer now that he has leaft the
building. Leaft, do you get it? Because he likes bushes.
Okay, item number six. Steve Bannon is also out. Now that's
out of the way, I want to tell you all a story about the
President.
                         (MORE)
                                              (CONTINUED)

CONTINUED:

                    HUCKABEE SANDERS (CONT'D)
Once upon a time, there was a little boy called Donald,
that's the President, only guys? Only back then he wasn't
running the country.

                              The ENSEMBLE begins to stand and
                              exit.

                    HUCKABEE SANDERS
Hey, where are you all going? I've not finished my story.
                    (following them)
He was a little boy, of only two hundred and thirty-nine
pounds, and he had a daddy, we all have a daddy, right? We
can relate?...

ACT II, SCENE THIRTEEN | TRUMP FINDS OUT ABOUT MUELLER

                              The OVAL OFFICE, where a large
                              office cupboard now stands next
                              to the desk.

                              The room is empty except for
                              ERIC, who sits alone on the
                              floor, attempting to play a
                              xylophone.

                    NARRATOR
                    (entering)
And so as the news spreads of Mueller's arrival, the
feeling among many is that the ending is final. With a
distinguished career as a veteran and attorney, Robert
Mueller is the man appointed special counsel to end Donald
Trump's journey. But the orange mango who is scared to ever
dance the foreign tango still remains in bliss, for he
watches Fox News' reports on burger emojis that make the
truth easy to miss. But how long can he remain outside the
know? As long as it takes Kellyanne Conway to ruin his
presidential flow.

                              The NARRATOR exits.

                                             (CONTINUED)
PERFORMANCE LICENSE EDITION   LICENSE # _ _ _ _ _ _ _

CONTINUED:

                              TRUMP
                           (entering)
Okay, Eric Trump, take it from the top. This is going to be
so great.

                    ERIC begins to play.

                              TRUMP
/OH DO NOT GO BREAKING MY NON-DISCLOSURE AGREEMENT./

                              ERIC
/I COULDN'T READ IT IF I TRIED./

                              TRUMP
/OH HONEY DO NOT TELL OUR STORY./

                              ERIC
/I FORGOT MY LINE./

                              TRUMP
/OH DO NOT GO BREAKING MY NON-DISCLOSURE AGREEMENT./

                              ERIC
/ESPECIALLY IF ON DAD YOU PEE./

                              TRUMP
/OH HONEY WHEN YOU KNOCK ON MY DOOR./

                              ERIC
/I FORGOT MY LINE./

            TRUMP   ERIC
/NOBODY KNOWS IT./   /(I DON'T KNOW ANYTHING.)/

                    CONWAY enters as ERIC stops
                    playing.

                             CONWAY
Mister President, sir, and oh, Eric too. I hope that I'm
not interrupting anything important?

                              TRUMP
No, Kellyanne Conway, it is okay. What did you want?

                                              (CONTINUED)

CONTINUED:

                         CONWAY
It's about the Russia investigation, sir. There's been a
new development.

                         TRUMP
What do you mean, the Russia investigation? There should
not be any Russia investigation. I fried James Comey.

                         CONWAY
Yes, you did, that's the problem. There are quite a few
people, including many in the Justice Department, who think
that you only fired him because he was investigating you.

                         TRUMP
That is fake news. I also fired him because he refused to
pledge loyalty to me, the great Pres...

                         CONWAY

President, sir?

                         TRUMP
Thank you, Kellyanne Conway. Even I find it hard to say
sometimes.

                         CONWAY
You finally have something in common with the world, sir.

                         TRUMP
As I was saying, I also fired him because he refused to
pledge loyalty to me, the great President Donald J. Trump.
Steve Bannon did it.

                         CONWAY
Well yes, but Steve Bannon has also recently left to start
a new job as the interactive trench foot exhibit in a war
museum. Anyway, it sounds crazy, the Justice Department is
using your admission to Sean Hannity that you fired James
Comey over the investigation as evidence that you fired
James Comey over the investigation. They've appointed a
special counsel.

                         TRUMP
Where was Jeff Sessions? Why did he not stop this?

                                                  (CONTINUED)

                    CONWAY
Jeff Sessions couldn't recall why he didn't stop it, but I
looked into it and found that he was busy selling a new
range of cookies at the store.

                         TRUMP moves over to his desk.

                    TRUMP
I have a great plan to solve this. I will just fire whoever
the special counsel is.

                              He sits, and the sound of a
                              whoopee cushion deflating fills
                              the stage before he stands and
                              holds it up.

                    ERIC
Dad made a naughty sound.

                    TRUMP
Kellyanne Conway, why is there a whoopee cushion on my
seat?

                    CONWAY
I don't know why, Mister President. Anyway, I'm not sure
that you can just fire the special counsel. It might not
look very good, and they've appointed someone who is quite
influential.

                    TRUMP
Who have they appointed, Kellyanne Conway?

                    CONWAY
                 (mumbling)
Robert Mueller.

                    TRUMP
Who?

                    CONWAY
Robert Mueller, sir.

                    TRUMP
Oh no.

                                             (CONTINUED)

>   Beat, and then TRUMP slowly sits
>   back down on the whoopee
>   cushion.

                    CONWAY
I share your concerns, sir.

                    TRUMP
This is not so great.

>   CONWAY pulls out her phone and
>   begins to look at it.

                    CONWAY
But you might be okay, Mister President. Looking on
Twitter, it doesn't look as though he has any evidence that
you've done anything illegal and **OH GOD!**

                    TRUMP
What is it, Kellyanne Conway?

                    CONWAY
It looks as though he's just found evidence that you've
done things that are illegal.

                    TRUMP
What evidence?

                    CONWAY
Don Junior has just tweeted the messages he received from
Julian Assange last year, and also the guest list for the
meeting with the Russians at Trump Tower.

>   JUNIOR enters.

                    JUNIOR
Hey dad, I was wondering if you could possibly help me out
by signing an executive order to ban some of the hotels
that I don't own.

                    TRUMP
Donald Trump Junior, why did you just tweet about getting
help from Julian Assange and also the Russia meeting?

                                        (CONTINUED)

CONTINUED:

                         JUNIOR
Oh, well about that... well, I don't know.

                         Beat.

                         ERIC
Hey dad, didn't you tweet about the Russia meeting too?

                              TRUMP pulls out his own phone as
                              ERIC begins to lick his the
                              mallet of his xylophone as
                              though it's a lolly.

                         JUNIOR
                       (to ERIC)
Hey buddy, that thing isn't for eating. It's for playing.
You're supposed to tap it like this.
                       (demonstrating)
Okay, you got it? Now you try.

                         ERIC plays a note.

                         ERIC
It makes a sound.

                         JUNIOR
It does make a sound, yes.

                              As JUNIOR turns away, ERIC
                              begins to tap his own head with
                              the mallet and make a sound each
                              time.

                         JUNIOR
                       (to TRUMP)
Dad, what are you doing?

                         TRUMP looks up from his phone.

                         TRUMP
I am blocking Robert Mueller on Twitter so that he cannot
see what I said about the Russia meeting.

                                               (CONTINUED)
PERFORMANCE LICENSE EDITION   LICENSE # _ _ _ _ _ _ _ _

JUNIOR
Why don't you just delete the tweets?

TRUMP
Because blocking people makes me feel excited in a way that
Melania has not made me feel for six years.

JUNIOR
You know, I don't think I should have eaten lunch before
coming to see you.

TRUMP
It is also fun and just so great to block people, like this
person, because she said that the Pope does not like me,
and this person because they said I upset a cute dog.
Retweeting is also so great, and so I am going to do it now
to this person who says they love what I am doing. Clearly,
they like me so much because they have a cross and a flag
in their bio and have rated me out of ten in their name.
MAGA girl two four nine six eight nine two seven. And now I
also block this person for saying I should delete my
account... oh, I already have Crooked Hillary Clinton
blocked.

                    HUCKABEE SANDERS enters.

HUCKABEE SANDERS
Mister President, hello, and hello to everyone else. I've
got a story to tell you all. I was in my office just a few
moments ago when two men arrived with a large package for
you, Mister President, and they wanted to know where to
deliver it.

TRUMP
Was it Vladimir Putin. Because I already have enough of
those teddy bears with eyes that move and a microphone for
a nose.

HUCKABEE SANDERS
No, sir. Robert Mueller --

                                              (CONTINUED)

                         TRUMP
                       (standing)
Quick, Eric Trump, Donald Trump Junior, close the curtains
and barricade all of the doors. Kellyanne Conway, you start
digging us an escape tunnel.

                    HUCKABEE SANDERS
I think you misunderstood me, sir. The package isn't Robert
Mueller, it's just from Robert Mueller. He sent it.

                         CONWAY
Mueller sent it? But what is it?

                    HUCKABEE SANDERS
I don't know, Kellyanne.

                         TRUMP
Have it brought in here.

                              HUCKABEE SANDERS exits and then
                              returns a moment later with two
                              DELIVERY MEN carrying a large
                              and flat wrapped package.

                         TRUMP
                   (pointing at his desk)
Place it on here.

                              After doing as instructed, the
                              DELIVERY MEN exit as TRUMP
                              unwraps the package, and all
                              (except ERIC) gather around.

                         JUNIOR
So you know, that looks like a portrait.

                              TRUMP holds it up to show a
                              portrait of Robert Mueller.

                         CONWAY
Okay, so does anyone think that it's suspicious that Robert
Mueller is sending a portrait of himself?

                                                 (CONTINUED)

                          TRUMP
Clearly, he is just sending it to show that there are no
hard feelings between us. He is a smart man, Kellyanne
Conway, and smart men often sent portraits of themselves to
show that they are smart.

                          CONWAY
I'm still suspicious of it, sir.

                          TRUMP
                    (ignoring CONWAY)
I think that it would look so great on this wall here.

                              He takes the portrait and puts
                              it up on the wall behind his
                              desk.

                          TRUMP
And now he can sit over me as my guardian angel of not
being under investigation.

                              As they all turn away from the
                              portrait, it 'opens' as if a
                              door and the real ROBERT MUELLER
                              appears and begins to listen to
                              the conversation.

                          CONWAY
But, Mister President, you are under investigation.

                          MUELLER nods.

                          TRUMP
Wrong. Robert Mueller would not have sent me a present if I
was under investigation.
                    (to JUNIOR)
Donald Trump Junior, can you go and get Mike Pence?

                          JUNIOR
Sure. I'll go get him for you right now.

                          JUNIOR exits.

                                                   (CONTINUED)

                         CONWAY
Mister Trump, I really think you should be talking to a
lawyer.

                         TRUMP
Okay, if you insist, Kellyanne Conway --

                              TRUMP turns to the cupboard next
                              to his desk as PENCE enters
                              wearing ear muffs.

                         PENCE
Mister President, sir. You asked to see me.

                         TRUMP
Mike Pence, why are you wearing ear muffs?

                              PENCE remains silent, and so
                              TRUMP walks over and lifts off
                              his ear muffs.

                         TRUMP
Mike Pence, I said, why are you wearing ear muffs?

                         PENCE
Because my lawyer advised me to wear them whenever I am
around you. He said that if I can't hear what you're
saying, then it's much easier to plead innocent.

                              PENCE puts the ear muffs back
                              on.

                         TRUMP
Mike Pence, we need your help.

                         Beat.

                         PENCE
I would love to stay and catch up with all of you, but if
none of you mind, I have my inauguration to start planning.

                         PENCE exits.

                                                  (CONTINUED)

                         TRUMP
Do you think he will invite all of us?

                         CONWAY
Mister Trump, you've got more important things to worry
about.

                         TRUMP
Quite right, Kellyanne Conway.

                                   TRUMP turns back to the
                                   cupboard.

                         CONWAY
What are you doing, sir?

                         TRUMP
I am calling Michael Cohen. Michael Cohen.

                                   The cupboard shakes for a moment
                                   then goes still before COHEN
                                   walks out of it.

                         COHEN
You called, boss?

                                   CONWAY and HUCKABEE SANDERS
                                   watch in shock while ERIC points
                                   with wonder.

                         ERIC
Magic trick.

                         CONWAY
What were you doing in a cupboard?

                         COHEN
Oh, it's where I live now, Kellyanne. I had to sell my
house to help get the boss out of some trouble.
                         (to TRUMP)
Nasty business with Robert Mueller. I've just heard more
news too, he's got Paul Manafort, the guy's in jail right
now.

                                                     (CONTINUED)

CONTINUED:

                         TRUMP
Who is Paul Manafort?

                         CONWAY
He used to get the coffee around here before I started.

                         TRUMP
Kellyanne Conway, go and send his family some flowers for
their loss, and also work on convincing one of his children
to start a fire in his filing cabinet.

                         CONWAY
I'll get straight to it, Mister President.

                    CONWAY exits.

                         TRUMP
So, Michael Cohen, what is your plan to get me out of this
investigation?

                         COHEN
I'm still working on coming up with something. Perhaps you
should consider hiring another lawyer to help?

                         TRUMP
I am already ahead of you, Michael Cohen.
                    (to HUCKABEE SANDERS)
Sarah Huckabee Sanders, can you go and find me Rudy
Giuliani?

                    HUCKABEE SANDERS
I can certainly do that for you, Mister President. It
sounds like it could be the start of a great adventure.

                    HUCKABEE SANDERS exits.

                         COHEN
About another matter, though, boss. I got a call earlier
from a guy. He claims to be a lawyer representing a Stormy
Daniels. You know, that porn star that you fu --

                         TRUMP
Michael Cohen, I am going to have to stop you there. There
is a child in the room.

                                             (CONTINUED)

                         COHEN
That porn start whose... missus Eric you stuck your mister
Eric in.

                         ERIC
Hey, that's an Eric kiss.

                              MUELLER coughs, and they look at
                              him.

                         MUELLER
Excuse me.

                         TRUMP
You are excused, Mister Robert Mueller.

                              They look away from Mueller.

                         COHEN
Anyway, boss, this guy said they're getting ready to sue
you because you never signed a non-disclosure agreement
with her.

                         TRUMP
That is fake news. I always sign non-disclosure agreements.
The only one that I have not signed is the one you gave me
before my speech last year, which I have right here...

                              He pulls the agreement from one
                              of the desk draws and begins to
                              look through it.

                         TRUMP
And this one is between Donald J. Trump and... what does
this say here, Michael Cohen?

                              COHEN moves closer.

                         COHEN
Stormy Daniels. It says Stormy Daniels and you forgot to
sign it. You told me that you never forgot to sign
anything.

                                                    (CONTINUED)

CONTINUED:

                         TRUMP
I do not remember saying that.

                         COHEN
Well, this could be a big problem, boss. This guy is a bald
guy, and no Breitbart reading kind neither. He may turn out
to be nearly as crooked as you some day, but he's got real
certificates. Not just those you get printed from some word
processor when you graduate Trump U.

                         TRUMP
Okay, we need a plan.

                    RUDY GIULIANI enters.

                         GIULIANI
Well, if you need a plan, then I am your man.

                         TRUMP
Rudy Giuliani.

                         GIULIANI
That's my name, and let me tell you... /YOU'VE GOT TROUBLE,
RIGHT HERE IN THIS OFFICE, I'M TALKING TROUBLE WITH A
CAPITAL T WHICH ALSO STANDS FOR TREASON./
                         (beat)
/BUT DON'T YOU WORRY, FOR SIR I HAVE A PLAN, WE'RE GOING TO
SAY TO EVERYONE ASKING THAT YOU'RE GUILTY./

                         TRUMP
I do not understand.

                         GIULIANI
/WE'RE GOING TO SAY THAT YOU'RE GUILTY./

                         COHEN
That he's guilty?

                         GIULIANI
/THAT HE'S GUILTY. WE SAY IT SO MUCH WE CONFUSE THEM ALL
INTO THINKING YOU'RE NOT./

                         COHEN
Into thinking that he's not guilty?

                                        (CONTINUED)

                    GIULIANI
/THAT'S RIGHT./

                    TRUMP
Why are you singing

                    GIULIANI
It's supposed to be a musical.

                    COHEN
No. It's supposed to be an alternative musical.

                    Beat.

                    COHEN
Boss, we still need to come up with a plan that might
actually work.

                    GIULIANI
I've just said, we're going to say he's guilty.

                    COHEN
But will it work, though?

                    TRUMP
Rudy Giuliani, will it work?

                    GIULIANI
Well, we've been saying it about Hillary Clinton for years,
and she's still not in jail.

                    TRUMP
Okay, Rudy Giuliani, I want you to go on all of the fake
news tonight and tell them that I am guilty. Michael Cohen,
I want you to take a shower because you smell like a not so
great bag of fried chicken, and then I want you to sort out
this Stormy Daniels problem.

                    GIULIANI
That's it, Donald, you've got it.

                    COHEN
Sure thing, boss.

                                              (CONTINUED)

CONTINUED:

> As COHEN and GIULIANI exit,
> TRUMP turns back to ERIC.

                    TRUMP
Okay, Eric Trump, whenever you are ready.

> ERIC begins to play.

                    TRUMP
/AND I THINK IT IS GOING TO BE A SHORT, SHORT TIME,
'TILL MUELLER INVESTIGATES ME AND FINDS,
I AM NOT THE MAN MY VOTERS THINK IS INNOCENT,
OH, NO, NO, NO. KIM JONG UN IS A ROCKET MAN.
SHORT, AND FAT, BURNING UP HIS COUNTRY ALL ALONE.../

> TRUMP exits as MUELLER looks
> down at ERIC and begins to
> smile.

ACT II, SCENE FOURTEEN | MUELLER INTERROGATES ERIC

> OUTSIDE THE WHITE HOUSE where a
> toy car is parked.

                    NARRATOR
                   (entering)
It would be true to say that across the administration, the
level of intelligence is not so high, but for one member,
it's lower and all who see him only sigh. But maybe his
family believe his heart is in the right place, even if he
struggles daily to tie up his own shoelace. Or perhaps it
is that he has to stay for he knows too much, a possibility
that some want to know if the case truly is as such. Eric
Trump has been the kid who has sat through every meeting
and seen exactly who his father has been greeting. But is
he loyal to his family name? Or can Robert Mueller use him
to his investigation's gain?

> ERIC enters and climbs into the
> car before he begins pushing
> himself around the stage, making
> engine noises.

                                        (CONTINUED)

> After a moment, the NARRATOR is
> joined by two FBI AGENTS, and
> together, they sneak up behind
> ERIC and push the car offstage.

                    ERIC (OFF)
Hey, where are you taking me? I'm the dumb one.

> Lights out, and for a moment,
> nothing, until a single
> spotlight goes up on ERIC on sat
> sitting opposite a desk.

                    ERIC
What's going on? I can see the light. Am I dead? I feel
like this looks like how dad describes a date.

                    FBI AGENT #1 (OFF)
Are you Eric Frederick Trump?

                    ERIC
No. I'm just Eric.

                    FBI AGENT #2 (OFF)
Are you the son of President Donald J. Trump?

                    ERIC
He prefers if we call him Lord Führer at home.

> The stage lights up to reveal an
> interrogation room.
>
> ERIC looks around as footsteps
> grow in volume until the two FBI
> AGENTS enter along with ROBERT
> MUELLER.

                    MUELLER
Mister Trump...

> He goes to shake ERIC'S hand,
> but rather than reciprocate,
> ERIC grabs and licks his.

                                        (CONTINUED)

CONTINUED:

                    MUELLER
Mister Trump, I am Robert Mueller.

                    He sits opposite ERIC.

                    ERIC
Son of a bitch.

                    MUELLER

I'm sorry?

                    ERIC

That's what dad calls you.

                    MUELLER
Well, that's who I wish to speak to you about today, Mister
Trump.

                    ERIC

I'm not allowed to talk to strangers.

                    MUELLER
Don't think of me as a stranger. Think of me as a distant
but kind uncle of yours.

                    ERIC

Can I have some candy?

                    MUELLER
I'm not sure I understand you, Mister Trump.

                    ERIC

I want candy. Uncles give candy.

                    MUELLER
Okay, I'm not that sort of uncle. I just want to ask you a
few questions and get a few answers.

                    ERIC

Can I have candy after?

                    MUELLER
                  (to FBI AGENTS)
Does either of you have some sweets we can give this kid?

                                        (CONTINUED)

PERFORMANCE LICENSE EDITION   LICENSE # _ _ _ _ _ _ _ _

> One of them reaches into their
> pocket and pulls out a bag of
> M&Ms to hand to ERIC.

FBI AGENT #1
I've only got these, sir.

ERIC
Uncle Mueller, I'm not allowed candy.

MUELLER
Well, I'm letting you have them as a special treat. Think
of me as a naughty uncle that lets you do things you
normally wouldn't be allowed to do.

ERIC
Like when dad asks Ivanka to call him an uncle, so it
sounds less creepy?

MUELLER
Mister Trump, I'm going to need you to swear an oath right
now that you're going to tell us the truth.

ERIC
I can't do that, Uncle Mueller. Junior says it's bad to
swear.

MUELLER
Look, Mister Trump, I just want to ask you about your
father and what he did during the election last year, and I
need you to promise that you'll tell the truth.

ERIC
Can we go eat pizza and watch a movie after?

MUELLER
Mister Trump, if you help us out here, then I promise that
I will personally arrange for you to meet the star of your
favorite movie.

ERIC
Cool. I've always wanted to meet a talking snowman.

(CONTINUED)

                         MUELLER
So do we have an arrangement?

                          ERIC
Okay, but I can't tell you about any of the stuff that dad
said I'm not allowed to talk about.

                         MUELLER
What did he say that you're not allowed to talk about?

                          ERIC
The help he got from the Russia meeting, Vladimir Putin
voting multiple times in Wisconsin, fake news online
attacking Hillary Clinton, and WikiLeaks hacking the D-N-C
for him.

                         MUELLER
Is there anything else he said you can't talk about?

                          ERIC
Future mom.

                         MUELLER
Who is future mom?

                          ERIC
She's the porn star that dad has Eric kisses with. But he
doesn't want anyone to know about her because his Uncle
Cohen paid her one hundred and thirty thousand dollars to
stay quiet.

                         MUELLER
One hundred and thirty thousand dollars? Why doesn't he
just use the internet like everyone else?

                          ERIC
Sometimes they only get paid one hundred and twenty
thousand.

                          Beat.

                                              (CONTINUED)

                         MUELLER
                      (to FBI AGENTS)
This kid is so stupid, I don't know whether to punch him or
kiss him for making our job easier.

                          ERIC
Don't kiss me. The doctor said it might be contagious.

                         MUELLER
Now, Mister Trump, you love your father, right?

                          ERIC
What is love?

                         MUELLER
Oh, love... well, love is what the majority of Americans
will be feeling towards me when I wrap up this
investigation.

                          ERIC
Will anyone ever feel love towards me?

                         MUELLER
I'm sure we can get you a pet if you want to try to
experience it yourself.

                          ERIC
No. I don't want a Reince Priebus.

                         MUELLER
I don't follow you, Mister Trump.

                          ERIC
That's what Uncle Scaramucci always called him. I miss
Uncle Scaramucci, but dad said he had to go away to a
better place.

                         MUELLER
I don't want to interrupt your story, Mister Trump, but I'd
quite like to wrap up this interview soon. So, I'm going to
ask you again, do you love your father?

                          ERIC
I think so.

                                                  (CONTINUED)

CONTINUED:

> MUELLER

Very good, that makes this easier. Now, there's a very good
chance that he's soon going to be locked up for a very long
time, do you understand me?

> ERIC

Is that like when he asks Ivanka to bring the chains?

> MUELLER

Back to your father being in jail, Mister Trump. I'm sure
that if you loved him, you wouldn't want him to be alone
for the rest of his life, would you?

> ERIC

No, but he could just get a mirror. That's what I do when I
want a friend to play with. I'm not talking to that friend
anymore, though. He said I look funny.

> MUELLER

Well, what we want to arrange for your father is something
similar to that, only with real people. His friends and his
family, for example. So can you help us out with that, so
he isn't alone?

> ERIC

Sure.

> MUELLER

So who do you think we should lock up with him for the
company? Anyone who has similar interests to him like
treason and sexual assault?

> ERIC

Well, there's Jared Kushner and Donald Trump Junior.

> MUELLER begins to note the names
> down.

> ERIC

Michael Cohen, Kellyanne Conway, Sean Spicer, Vladimir
Putin, Ivanka Trump, Eric Trump, Michael Flynn, Stephen
Miller, Steve Bannon, Rudy Giuliani, Jeff Sessions,
European mom, and a some guy named George.

(CONTINUED)

                         Beat.

                         MUELLER
                    (to FBI AGENTS)
Look at this kid.
                    (to ERIC)
Well, Mister Trump, that's all that I need to ask you.
You've been a big help to me and your country.

                         ERIC
Do I get to meet a talking snowman now?

                         MUELLER
Meet a talking snowman?... Well, I'll tell you what, if you
come back here next week, you can meet one, okay? But just
remember to bring your father and your brother too, you
wouldn't want them to miss out now, would you?

                         ERIC
What about Jared Kushner?

                         MUELLER
Now you're getting it. Well, run along then and tell them
all the exciting news.

                         ERIC
Thank you, Uncle Mueller. I love you.

                         MUELLER
And right now, I love you too, kid.

                         ERIC begins walking offstage.

                         MUELLER
The exit is the other way, Mister Trump.

                         ERIC
I knew that.

                         He changes direction and exits.

                         MUELLER stands and puts his arms
                         around the FBI AGENTS.

                                        (CONTINUED)
PERFORMANCE LICENSE EDITION   LICENSE # _ _ _ _ _ _ _ _

                         MUELLER
You know, I think we can go out and celebrate tonight. I
think we've got those treasonous assholes.

ACT II, SCENE FIFTEEN | MICHAEL COHEN FLIPS

                              The OVAL OFFICE, where JUNIOR
                              sits tied to a chair while TRUMP
                              is taunting him by holding
                              hairspray just out of reach.

                         NARRATOR
                         (entering)
With now in hand the knowledge that from Eric Trump he did
demand, Robert Mueller sets forth to have his team raid
offices from the south, east, west, and to the north.
Lawyers, secretaries, and a tea boy too, Flynn, Manafort,
and Michael Cohen, to name just a few. The net is now
closing fast around the President, and many around him know
exactly by this what is meant. Every other day a new name
jumps ship, and with a lifeboat ready sits Mueller if they
promise to talk from their lip. But with a team of lawyers
working to work the lies which they mill, Donald Trump sits
confident of being found innocent somehow even still. Sure
his son Junior shared on Twitter evidence and more, but
that is why now he sits tied to a chair on the Oval Office
floor. For his father to solve it is still sure of his
plan, but then still little does he know he's about to lose
his favorite lawyer man.

                         The NARRATOR exits.

                         TRUMP
You are not getting your hairspray back until you have sent
that tweet, Donald Trump Junior.

                         JUNIOR
But dad, if I don't spray my hair at least once an hour,
then I end up looking like you.

                                                (CONTINUED)

                         TRUMP
Then pull out your phone and get tweeting, otherwise I will
leave you tied up and make you babysit your brother
tonight, and just a little F-Y-I, we have not changed his
diaper.

                         JUNIOR
Okay, fine.

                    He pulls out his phone.

                         JUNIOR
                    (to himself, reading)
"I welcome this opportunity to share this statement to set
out the circumstances around the reported Russia meeting at
Trump Tower last year."
                    (to TRUMP)
What do you want me to say?

                         TRUMP
It has been reported by the lying fake news media that I
met with Russia. I did meet with Russia, but nothing
happened, and I did not do anything illegal. If I did do
anything illegal, then it was the fault of Crooked Hillary
Clinton. P-S, my father was not at the meeting.

                    COHEN enters.

                         COHEN
You know, boss, you're wasting your time. There's no point
in trying to fight it.

                         TRUMP
What are you talking about, Michael Cohen?

                         COHEN
I'm talking about how it's not going to make a difference.
Everyone already knows about that Russia meeting and
everything that happened at it. You tweeted about it, Don
Junior tweeted about it, and Comrade Putin even set a photo
from it as the header of the Kremlin's profile.

                                                  (CONTINUED)

                         TRUMP
I am not worried, Michael Cohen. We are just going to deny
the Russia meeting, and then they have no more evidence.

                         COHEN
I wouldn't be sure of that, boss. Last I heard, Robert
Mueller sat down with one of your children the other day
and asked some questions.

                         TRUMP
None of them would be stupid enough to have told the truth.

                         COHEN
It was Eric Trump.

                         Beat.

                         TRUMP
We are so screwed.

                         COHEN
Exactly, boss. Robert Mueller now has all the evidence he
needs.

                         TRUMP
I still do not need to worry. I still have you as my
lawyer, and as long as you are here, there will always be
someone to pay the bribes to get me out of any situation.

                         COHEN
Well actually, about that, boss. I've come to hand in my
resignation to you. I've been speaking to the Mueller team,
and they've offered me an out. I want to flip.

                         TRUMP
You do not get an out, Michael Cohen. No one in this
administration gets a way out. There are no redemptions
from this.

                    GIULIANI enters.

                         TRUMP
Rudy Giuliani, have you heard this? Michael Cohen says he
is going to flip.

                                             (CONTINUED)

                              GIULIANI grabs COHEN by the
                              head.

                         GIULIANI
I'm sure he's just having a joke with us.

                          COHEN
Hey, get off me. I'm not joking around here.

                              COHEN breaks free.

                          COHEN
They came and raided my office this morning and found
evidence of everything. There's nothing more I can do for
you now, and I don't think there's anything you can do
either, boss.

                          TRUMP
What are you saying, Michael Cohen?

                          COHEN
I'm saying that right now, I'm pretty sure there's a Stormy
coming right for you.

                              Beat.

                          TRUMP
Please, Michael Cohen. There must still be something that
you can do for me?

                          COHEN
Mister Trump, I'm not even a real lawyer. I couldn't even
get a place at Trump U. I had to get my degree from Trump U
Junior.

                          TRUMP
I can offer you money. I can offer you lots of great green
American dirty bribe money.

                          COHEN
Boss, you still haven't paid me back for paying off all
those lawsuits for you. Besides, Robert Mueller has offered
me something you never could.
                         (MORE)

                                              (CONTINUED)

CONTINUED:

                         COHEN (CONT'D)
A nice comfortable cell where I get three meals a day, new
clothes, and never have to speak to another member of the
public ever again.

                         TRUMP
Please, Michael Cohen. Stay and help me.

                         COHEN
No, Mister Trump. This is the end. It's over. You've never
respected me, and the other lawyers bully me --

                         GIULIANI
That's not true.

                         COHEN
Yes, it is. You always steal my lunch money, and you even
wrote to the President of the Bar Association to tell her I
have posters of her on my bedroom walls.

                         GIULIANI
It was a good joke.

                         COHEN
I don't even have a bedroom. I have to live in a bush now
because the boss evicted me from my cupboard.

                         TRUMP
It was prime real estate, Michael Cohen. You know that.

                         COHEN
Have you got any idea what it's like to have Sean Spicer as
a roommate?

                         TRUMP
What about if I give you your cupboard back?

                         COHEN
It's too late. Robert Mueller is going to bring you and
everyone around you down. And you know what, I'm going to
help them as much as I can. You're a bad man, Mister Trump,
and everyone is going to find out what you've done to their
country. You're not the boss of me anymore... boss.

                                                  (CONTINUED)

> Beat, and then COHEN exits as
> CONWAY and ERIC enter.

CONWAY

Mister President, do you need a moment? That looked as
though it was emotional.

TRUMP

Kellyanne Conway, we just lost a very fine, and a very
great, member of our catering team.

CONWAY

Well anyway, sir, I think that we're going to need to come
up with a new idea.

GIULIANI

What's wrong with my idea? It's working. We've told
everyone that the President is guilty and he's not been
arrested yet.

CONWAY

Yet.

GIULIANI

They can't arrest a sitting president. They wouldn't try.

CONWAY

No, but they can wait until he's not a sitting president.
And they can also arrest all of us now.

GIULIANI

Then we will them that we're all guilty. That everyone is
guilty. What are they going to do about it? Arrest all of
us?

CONWAY

They are trying to. Just last week, they indicted twelve
household cleaners, eleven gardeners gardening, ten lawyers
lying, nine drivers driving, eight butlers buttling, seven
librarians reading, six stewards seating, five-clothes-
valets, four table waiters, three bell boys, two tea
blenders and the former campaign barista.

> ERIC begins to clap.

(CONTINUED)

CONTINUED:

                              CONWAY
                           (to ERIC)
Thank you.

                           (to TRUMP)
So you see, sir, I really think we need to try doing
something different.

                              TRUMP
Have we tried calling it all a witch hunt in the hope that
it makes it just go away? Or we use thoughts and prayers?

                              CONWAY
We only use thoughts and prayers for problems we could
actually fix if we wanted to, sir.

                              TRUMP
What about paper towels? Have we tried paper towels?

                              CONWAY
Paper towels don't really do anything, sir... ever.

                              TRUMP
What about Jeff Sessions? Why can't he just close down the
investigation?

                              CONWAY
Oh, about Jeff Sessions. I saw him earlier, and he said he
was planning on coming to see you, but he's going to have
to reschedule because he's got to spend the day trying to
recall which rainbow he left his pot of gold at the end of.

Also, Mister President, if you don't mind me asking, why is
Donald Trump Junior tied to a chair?

                              JUNIOR
Can someone untie me now?

                              TRUMP
I cannot let you out, Donald Trump Junior. I used a lock
and gave the key to Eric Trump to keep it safe.

                    They all look to ERIC.

                                                    (CONTINUED)

                         ERIC
That was a key? I thought it was candy.

                    KUSHNER enters.

                         CONWAY
So what are we going to do about Robert Mueller, sir?

                         TRUMP
Jared Kushner, do you have any ideas?

                    KUSHNER holds up a cue card.

                         CONWAY
                    (reading)
"No. I have no idea about anything and don't know why I'm
still here."
                    (beat)
Jared Kushner has no idea about anything and doesn't know
why he's still here, sir.

                         ERIC
Why don't we just run away?

                         GIULIANI
The kid has a point. Running away could work.

                         TRUMP
Kellyanne Conway, what language do they speak in South
America?

                         CONWAY
They speak Spanish in many places, sir. Why do you ask?

                         TRUMP
Puedo hablar Español.

                         CONWAY
Mister President?

                         TRUMP
I said I can speak Spanish. My father taught it to me when
I was a little boy and told me that if I ever get into
trouble, then I should run away to South America.

                                        (CONTINUED)

PERFORMANCE LICENSE EDITION   LICENSE # _ _ _ _ _ _ _ _

CONTINUED:

                         CONWAY
But what about your children, sir?

                         JUNIOR
Yo tambien puedo hablar Español.

                         TRUMP
Donald Trump Junior and Ivanka Trump are both fluent. Even
Eric Trump knows some words.

                         ERIC
Guten tag.

                         CONWAY
Mister President, are you suggesting that we just leave all
of this behind? That we just run away from the mess we've
created so that someone else has to clean it up?

                         TRUMP
Yes, I am.

                         CONWAY
I'm in. What do we do?

                         TRUMP
Rudy Giuliani, I need you to stay behind and make sure that
no one knows we have gone anywhere.

                         GIULIANI
I can do that, and when they come after me, I'll just tell
them that I'm guilty. What's the worst they can do?

                         CONWAY
Prosecute you for treason.

                         GIULIANI
They only prosecute you if they like you, Kellyanne.

                         TRUMP
Donald Trump Junior, you are going to stay tied to that
chair until we can get the key back.

                                                   (CONTINUED)

CONTINUED:

                              JUNIOR
Why can't we just tell Eric where babies come from so he
brings it back up straight away?

                              ERIC
I already know where babies come from. The baby fairy puts
them under your pillow at night.

                              TRUMP
                         (to JUNIOR)
Because no one wants to clean up that mess.
                         (to CONWAY)
Kellyanne Conway, I need you to go and get Ivanka Trump,
and also some glasses and some fake mustaches, and then
meet us at the airport in one hour.

                              CONWAY
Mister President, just one thing, sir. I really like this
plan, okay, but don't we need to leave someone behind to
take the blame for us.

                              TRUMP
Kellyanne Conway, I have already thought about this, and I
know of such a great goat.

                              Slowly, they all turn to stare
                              at KUSHNER, who, after staring
                              back for a moment, turns around
                              his cue card to reveal, "Why are
                              you all looking at me?"

ACT II, SCENE SIXTEEN | THE ESCAPE TO SOUTH AMERICA

                              An AIRPORT TERMINAL where
                              CONWAY, ERIC, IVANKA, and TRUMP,
                              along with JUNIOR (still tied to
                              a chair), all of them are
                              wearing glasses and a fake
                              mustache, are talking to a CHECK-
                              IN agent.

                                              (CONTINUED)

                          NARRATOR
                         (entering)
And so with Cohen having flipped, next comes the inevitable
sinking of the ship. The days of freedom are now limited
for those at the top, and they know they have no choice but
to flee from the chop. Donald J. Trump with two of his sons
and Ivanka too, along with Kellyanne Conway, who completes
their few. Mike Pence has already fled the nest, and not
one of them cares who is arrested from the rest.

                                   The NARRATOR exits as HANNITY
                                   enters but stands to watch from
                                   the side.

                          TRUMP
Hello check-in person, we are here for the flight to South
America even though I hear it is overrated. There is five
of us.
                         (looking around)
Make that four of us, we should probably check Donald Trump
Junior in as baggage because we still cannot untie him.

                          ERIC
I haven't been for poo-poo yet.

                          CHECK-IN AGENT
And do any of you have a preference of where you'd like to
sit on the plane?

                          TRUMP
As far along the right-wing as possible.

                          CHECK-IN AGENT
And other than this chair, do you have any baggage to
check?

                          CONWAY
I might need to pay some excess charges here. I've picked
up a lot since I started working for Mister Trump.

                                   The CHECK-IN AGENT hands over
                                   their boarding passes.

                                                      (CONTINUED)

                    CHECK-IN AGENT
Here are your boarding passes, and if you'd like to make
your way through security, boarding will begin in just over
an hour.

                    TRUMP
Eric Trump, make sure you have your clear school bag ready
for security to check.

                         The CHECK-IN AGENT moves to push
                         JUNIOR offstage.

                    IVANKA
Daddy, why isn't Jared Kushner coming?

                    TRUMP
Jared Kushner was a great guy, but... Kellyanne Conway, can
you take this one?

                    CONWAY
Sure thing, Mister Trump.
                         (putting her arm around
                         IVANKA)
Ivanka, let me tell you a story about how there are plenty
more fish in the South American Sea.

                         CONWAY and IVANKA exit.

                    ERIC
Hey, where's European mom?

                    TRUMP
She said she's having dinner with a lawyer tonight.

                         Beat, and then HANNITY
                         approaches them.

                    HANNITY
Donald J. Trump.

                         TRUMP turns to him.

                    TRUMP
Sean Hannity.

                                        (CONTINUED)

                          ERIC
Dad, are we going away for a long time? Because Uncle
Mueller promised that he would introduce us all to a
talking snowman.

                          TRUMP
Eric Trump, if you are good and leave us alone, I will buy
you a talking snowman toy from the shop.

                          ERIC
I can be a good boy. If I try hard, I can even be a real
boy.

                    ERIC exits.

                          HANNITY
President Trump, sir.

                          TRUMP
Sean Hannity.

                          HANNITY
Does it have to end this way? I thought that we were all
going to grow old together in prison. You, me, and everyone
else. I thought Betsy DeVos would count her days in prison
in elephants.

                          TRUMP
You could come with us, Sean Hannity. It would be great.

                          HANNITY
But if I leave, who will look after Tucker Carlson? He
needs me as a role model otherwise, he might grow up to be
a respected journalist.

                          TRUMP
You do such fantastic work with that man, Sean Hannity.

                          HANNITY
Will I ever see you again?

                                              (CONTINUED)

TRUMP
Of course, you will see me again. You will see my face
every day on all of the wanted posters. They are going to
be <u>huge</u>.

HANNITY watches as TRUMP exits.

HANNITY
You were a good friend, Mister President.

A moment, and then HANNITY takes
a deep breath as PUTIN enters
and places his arm around his
shoulders.

PUTIN
Don't not worry about Donald. Tell me, how you like to be
world leader in year two thousand and twenty?

Together, they exit.

ACT II, SCENE SEVENTEEN | KUSHNER IN THE OVAL OFFICE

The OVAL OFFICE, where KUSHNER
sits alone behind the desk
looking around confused and
scared.

NARRATOR
(entering)
And so we reach at last the end of our first part, and
still yet to show Trump is any sign of a heart. And so
while to South America he now takes flight, there is
another who sits in the Oval Office on this night. For it
is that Jared Kushner, in all the commotion, has received
an unexpected promotion. From the bottom to the top, being
president is now his job. But little is Jared aware of just
how badly he is about to fare.

The NARRATOR exits.

(CONTINUED)

>   For a moment, KUSHNER continues
>   to look around, and then
>   suddenly, there's loud banging
>   and lights fill the stage as the
>   ENSEMBLE (as FBI AGENTS) storm
>   on stage and surround him.

                         FBI AGENT #1
We're looking for the President.

>   Beat, and then KUSHNER begins to
>   raise his hands.

                         KUSHNER
I want my mommy.

>   Lights out.

<u>END OF PART ONE</u>

Lightning Source UK Ltd.
Milton Keynes UK
UKHW030857191120
373690UK00009B/663